A swarm of death . . .

Something hard slapped Johnn

and then another and another

kind of locust, brown and brittle. Johnny swatted them—and they exploded into ashy gray powder. They stank of mildew and decay. He clenched his teeth to keep from shrieking in terror—to keep the horrible, scratchy, swarming things from scrambling right into his mouth.

They were dead! *The millions of flying things were only shells, dry and hollow—and yet their wings buzzed and the creatures piled on, more and more, their dead legs scratching and scrabbling over his flesh, a maddening prickle over every inch of his exposed skin. . . .*

"This book has it all—supernatural spells, an evil sorcerer, horror, and several brushes with death. Fantasy-mystery lovers will enjoy the fast pace and creepy details."

—*Booklist*

DISCOVER THE TERRIFYING WORLD OF JOHN BELLAIRS!

John Bellairs's Johnny Dixon in

THE BELL,
THE BOOK,
AND
THE SPELLBINDER

BY

BRAD STRICKLAND

Frontispiece
by Edward Gorey

PUFFIN BOOKS

PUFFIN BOOKS
Published by the Penguin Group
Penguin Putnam Books for Young Readers,
345 Hudson Street, New York, New York 10014, U.S.A.
Penguin Books Ltd, 27 Wrights Lane, London W8 5TZ, England
Penguin Books Australia Ltd, Ringwood, Victoria, Australia
Penguin Books Canada Ltd, 10 Alcorn Avenue, Toronto, Ontario, Canada M4V 3B2
Penguin Books (N.Z.) Ltd, 182-190 Wairau Road, Auckland 10, New Zealand

Penguin Books Ltd, Registered Offices: Harmondsworth, Middlesex, England

First published in the United States of America by Dial Books for Young Readers,
a division of Penguin Books USA Inc., 1997
Published by Puffin Books,
a member of Penguin Putnam Books for Young Readers, 2000

1 3 5 7 9 10 8 6 4 2

THE LIBRARY OF CONGRESS HAS CATALOGED THE DIAL EDITION AS FOLLOWS:
Strickland, Brad.
The bell, the book, and the spellbinder / by Brad Strickland
frontispiece by Edward Gorey.
p. cm.
Based on the characters of John Bellairs
Summary: When Fergie falls under the spell of an evil sorcerer, Johnny Dixon and
Professor Childermass risk their own lives to save him.
ISBN 0-8037-1831-4 (tr.)
[1. Magic—Fiction. 2. Wizards—Fiction.]
I. Bellairs, John. II. Gorey, Edward, date, ill. III. Title IV. Title: John Bellairs's
Johnny Dixon in
PZ7.S9166Be 1997 [Fic]—dc20 96-41678 CIP AC

Puffin Books ISBN 0-14-130362-X

Printed in the United States of America

For Jonathan Abucejo and Steve Ericson,
defenders of the faith

CHAPTER ONE

"All right," said Johnny Dixon. "I've got one."

Byron Q. Ferguson—better known as "Fergie"—said, "Okay. What are their initials?"

Johnny, a pale, blond boy of about thirteen, pulled his glasses down on his nose and peered at Fergie over the gold wire rims, as Mrs. Pumbleton, Fergie's English teacher, often did. "Now, Byron," he said in a loopy, high-pitched voice, "there are both a horse *and* a rider, so that really should count as two questions."

"Okay, okay," groused Fergie, but he couldn't help grinning. Johnny did a pretty good impression of Mrs. Pumbleton, and it rarely failed to make Fergie smile. He was taller than Johnny, with jug ears, curly black hair, sleepy eyes, a long, droopy face, and big feet. The boys were about the same age, though they were very different in other ways. Johnny was timid and Fergie was bold. Johnny had to struggle at sports and Fergie was a natural athlete. Today Johnny wore his red windbreaker, blue corduroy pants, and black sneakers, and Fergie was wearing his motorcycle outfit: skintight jeans, a white T-shirt, and a black leather jacket decorated with metal and glass studs. But even though they were so different, they had become good friends since meeting at a Boy Scout camp a couple of years earlier. Fergie squirmed and muttered, "Okay, if you wanna be cheap with the clues, just give me the rider's initials."

Johnny grinned. "Hm. I guess that would have to be A.T.G."

"Aw, Dixon," complained his friend, "why don't you come up with a hard one? That's kid stuff. Alexander the Great, and the horse is Bucephalus."

"Rats—you're right," said Johnny. "That's twenty-seven for you, twenty-four for me. Your turn."

It was a rainy March afternoon in the mid-1950's. The two friends sat at a table in the Conversation Room of the public library. They were playing a game they had made up themselves, called "horse and rider." Each one had a chance to think up the names of a horse and rider from history or literature. The other could ask five questions, and then he had to guess the names of the horse and rider. If he got the answer after one question, he received five points, but if it took him two questions, he got four. A player who had to ask all five questions got only one point, but if he could not identify the horse and rider, he had to give up five whole points. It took a couple of real fanatics about trivia and history to make up and enjoy such a game.

Fergie looked out the window. The gray, cold day and the dismal rain did little to make the small town of Duston Heights, Massachusetts, look inviting. Trees with small, bright-green spring leaves drooped and dripped, and the gutters in the streets swirled with rushing, foamy rivulets. "I'm tired of this game," complained Fergie.

"Well, you can't quit while you're ahead. I've got another turn coming."

"Okay, okay, keep your hair on your head for a minute." Fergie yawned. He glared at the gray window, crawling with raindrops, and drummed his fingers impatiently on the library table. "Man, oh, man, I just wish there was something to *do*."

Johnny shrugged. "We could check out some books."

Making a sour face, Fergie said, "Aw, Dixon, I think between us we've already read every last book in this crummy library."

For a little while the two friends just sat silently, with Fergie staring out the window as he tried to dream up a horse and rider that would stump Johnny. Johnny suddenly said, "You know, I wonder what that is."

Fergie blinked. "What *what* is?"

"The last book in the library," replied Johnny. "I mean, the very last one in the whole place."

"You're outa your jug, John baby," said Fergie with a grin. "That's a pretty weird thing to wonder."

"I just meant—" began Johnny.

Fergie interrupted him, "Okay. I got one. Go ahead."

Johnny considered. "Are they real or imaginary?"

"Real," said Fergie. "One down."

"From American history?" asked Johnny.

"Yup," Fergie said. "You'll never get it in a million years."

"Robert E. Lee and Traveler," said Johnny.

"Oh, man!" Fergie rolled his eyes. "Okay, John baby, that's twenty-eight for you. I give up. You win. But tell me one thing—how'd ya ever guess it? Were you like reading my brainwaves or something?"

Johnny chuckled. "Elementary, my good Watson. You *always* bring in Robert E. Lee and Traveler at least once. I figured you'd think that I'd think you wouldn't go for something obvious, so you went for something obvious. But what you didn't know is that I knew you didn't know that I knew you'd go for something obvious."

"I'll stop you the very second you start making sense," muttered Fergie.

"No, it's just psychology. Really simple when you know how to do it. It's just like in Edgar Allan Poe's story 'The Purloined Letter,' " said Johnny.

"Yeah, yeah. The great detective C. Auguste Dupin an' all that stuff." Fergie yawned again, even wider than before. "Dixon, we gotta think up something to do. I am bored out of my skull!"

"Hey, look at the time," said Johnny, glancing at his wristwatch. "It's almost five o'clock. I have to get home. Gramma and Grampa are having Professor Childermass over for dinner tonight."

"An' they didn't invite me?" Fergie said, making his

lower lip tremble. "My little heart is broken. Boo, hoo, hoo."

Johnny had jumped up from his chair. He paused with his hand on the chair back, his expression anxious. "Fergie, you know you can come too. Gramma and Grampa wouldn't mind."

Fergie laughed at the look of concern on Johnny's face. "Come on, Dixon, I'm just pullin' your leg. Go ahead an' stuff your face with the prof an' your folks. I don't mind. I'm gonna snoop around an' see if there's anything I haven't read yet. Hey, you an' Sarah want to get together with me on Saturday to play flies an' grounders? If it stops rainin', I mean."

Johnny made a face. "If it *doesn't*, I think we better start to build an ark. See ya."

"Yeah, see ya." For a little while after Johnny left, Fergie just sat there, staring at the rain and wishing he were somewhere else. Anywhere else. He didn't much want to go home. His dad was a traveling salesman, and he was good at his job. Mr. Ferguson was a short, bald man who looked sort of timid and quiet, but people really liked him, and he had a reputation for honesty. In the last few years Mr. Ferguson had earned enough money to move the family from a cheap railroad apartment to a nice little house on the edge of Cranbrook, the snooty neighborhood of Duston Heights. Still, Fergie's dad was away from home a lot. Like now, for instance. He was on the road somewhere up in Vermont or New Hampshire, and he wouldn't be back for another week or so.

Mrs. Ferguson was at home, of course, but Fergie's mom made him nervous because she was always worrying about him and asking him questions. Mrs. Ferguson read a lot of magazine quizzes with titles like "Is Your Son Going Bad?" and "Ten Ways to Tell If Your Child Is a Juvenile Delinquent." Fergie's mom had the idea that her only son might be turning into a young hoodlum. Sometimes Fergie thought it was fun to kid her along about that—for instance, he recently had bought a comb that folded up to look exactly like a switchblade knife. She had just about had a fit when she found it in his jeans pocket. Fergie chuckled at the memory of how she held the thing between her forefinger and thumb, as if it were something dirty, and demanded an explanation. When he took the comb from her, flipped it open, and ran it through his hair, her stunned expression had been hilarious.

Oh, there were times when Fergie liked his mom and dad just the way they were. He knew how hard his dad worked, and he knew that his mom's worrying was what any mother would do. But at other times, Fergie wished he and his family were more, well, normal. Mrs. Ferguson was even more jittery when her husband was on a sales trip and the weather was bad. Right now Fergie didn't want to go home and have his mom nervously ask him questions about where he'd been and who had been with him.

Yet when Fergie thought about it, he had to admit he had it a little better than Dixon. Johnny's mom had died of cancer years before, and his father was an Air Force pilot who was practically never home. Still, when Major Dixon *did* visit, he and Johnny did neat stuff together. Last Christmas they had gone deep-sea fishing in Florida. Fergie's dad was kind and considerate, but he always seemed tired and almost never did things with Fergie. They only rarely fished in the ponds around Duston Heights, and Mr. Ferguson would never dream of going after tarpon in the Gulf of Mexico.

On this dark, drippy day, thinking about his mom and dad just made Fergie glum. He took a deep breath, noticing the library smells of dusty books, floor polish, and furniture wax. A Waterbury wall clock ticked slowly, clacking the seconds away. "I wonder what the last book in the library really is," murmured Fergie. Well, finding out was something to do, at least. He pushed his chair back and walked past the circulation desk, where Mrs. Medford, a chubby, cheerful librarian, didn't even look up. He climbed the stairs to the top floor.

It was even more gloomy up there, with narrow windows and only a few light fixtures giving a feeble yellow illumination. Fergie went past the histories and biographies. He went all the way to the very last set of shelves. These stood within just a couple of feet of a blank wall, making a kind of dark little alley. Fergie thought that a large person would never have been able to fit between the wall and the shelf, although he had no trouble. "Huh," he said, squatting to peer at the bottom shelf. The shadows made it hard to see, but Fergie's eyes slowly adjusted. A fat, dull-looking book was there, its title stamped on the spine in faded gold lettering: *A Genealogist in Providence*. The Dewey decimal number was below that: 999.99 S. Fergie pulled it out, wrinkling his nose. It looked crummy enough.

Anyway, he decided after flipping through it, it was nothing he wanted to read. He started to return the book to its place, and then he noticed something he hadn't before. Another book was there. The one he held was only the second to last book in the library. The real last one was thin and narrow. Fergie pulled it out. It came in a cloud of dust, dry and sharp, tickling his nose like pepper. He sneezed, a blasting *ahhh-chooo!* that echoed in the stacks.

"Bless you, boy."

Fergie jumped a mile. He tottered up to his feet and turned, his left shoulder hitting the wall. "Wow! You sc—I mean, you surprised me!"

At the end of the row of shelves stood a skinny little man. He was bald on top, with a long fringe of curling white hair spreading over the shoulders of his ankle-length black coat. His face was pink, with two bright blue eyes, a sharp nose, and a thin-lipped mouth. The man smiled in apology, showing white teeth that gleamed in the dimness. His voice was soft, like the purr of a big cat, with a faint trace of a British accent. "I am sorry. I didn't mean to. It looks as if you have discovered a very interesting volume there."

Fergie looked down at the book in his hands. The last book in the library had a battered black cloth cover, and on the front was a red rectangle with the title lettering inside, also as red as blood:

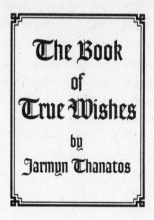

The Book
of
True Wishes
by
Jarmyn Thanatos

For some reason, Fergie shivered as he read those words. And just then something strange happened. From somewhere came the loud, solemn pealing of a huge bell, like the kind of great church bell called a bourdon. The sound tolled so near that Fergie felt the floor beneath his feet vibrate. It was only one loud, long *bo-o-o-n-ng*, but it seemed to go on forever.

"Time to go," the man said. "I wish you good reading, my young friend." He turned and walked away.

"Hey, wait," Fergie said weakly, but the man gave no sign of hearing him. Fergie felt a little dizzy. And he wondered about that loud bell. Where had the sound come from? No church was close enough to produce that kind of peal, and anyway, church bells didn't ring at five-twenty on Thursday afternoons. It hadn't been a clock bell, because no clock would ring at twenty minutes past the hour. "This is screwy," muttered Fergie to himself.

Fergie opened the book and looked at the title page. It just repeated the title and the author's name, Jarmyn Thanatos. He turned to the first page of the book, noticing that the pages were printed on very thin slick paper, so that it was easy to turn over two when you meant to turn only one. His eye fell on the first two paragraphs:

> Once there was a boy much like you. He was smarter and stronger and braver than everyone else, and most people secretly disliked him because he always spoke his mind and told the truth. He often wished that his family and friends appreciated him more. Then one day he found a wonderful book that made all his wishes come true—just as you have found this book.
>
> You can have everything that you want, Fergie. Your father can stay home and become a rich man. And you will be the one who makes that possible!

"Holy cow!" said Fergie. He shivered. How in the world did his name get in this crazy book? Man, he *had* to read this. He opened the back cover and stared.

To check out a book in the Duston Heights Library, you signed your name on a lined blue card tucked into a paper pocket glued to the inside back cover. Only, this book had no checkout card. Instead, printed inside the back cover, in the same red letters as the title on the front, were the words:

Fergie, Take Me Home

"I think I was wrong," Fergie told himself. "Dixon isn't outa his jug. I'm outa mine!"

But he stuffed the book inside the front of his jacket. It made him feel funny, because despite his mom's fears, Fergie was a good kid. He had never stolen anything in his life. But now he felt like a thief as he hurried downstairs, rushed past the circulation desk, and went out into the rain. It pelted his head and face. "Oh, great," Fergie mumbled. The cold rain made him hunch deep into his leather jacket. He started to trot along the street, heading for home.

"Young man!"

Fergie stopped, his heart leaping into his throat. He was in for it now! Somebody had caught him. He turned slowly. Ten feet away, under a store awning, stood the skinny little old man he had seen in the library. "Y-yeah?" Fergie said, trying to sound tough.

The old man smiled. "Keep your library book dry under that jacket. Snake eyes," he said. "I like it very much."

For a minute, Fergie didn't know what he was talking about. Then he remembered the decoration on the back of his leather jacket. It was a skull, with glowing red reflector studs for eyes. Above the skull were the words "Snake Eyes."

"Yeah," Fergie said. "Well, I gotta go."

"Yes," the man said. "It *is* later than you think."

And for the second time, the echoing peal of a bell rolled through the streets, coming from nowhere and everywhere. It made Fergie jump like a sudden blast of thunder, and it launched him into an all-out run. He didn't stop until he got home. Then he locked himself in his room and took a closer look at that very, very strange volume he had stolen from the library.

CHAPTER TWO

The sun broke through the clouds on Friday afternoon. Johnny and his friend Sarah Channing came out of St. Michael's School at three-thirty under a clearing sky. "Hooray," said Sarah, a tall, red-haired girl who was more at home in jeans and sweatshirts than in dresses. Today, though, she wore a school outfit—a green plaid skirt, white blouse, and scuffed brown shoes. "Looks like we're not going to float away after all."

"I hope it warms up," said Johnny, shivering a little. The wind was cold. "Want to stop at Peter's Sweet Shop? Fergie might show up."

"Okay," said Sarah. They walked to the confectionery store and bought a couple of chocolate malteds. They sat in a booth toward the front, where the afternoon sun warmed them. Now and again the shadow of a cloud suddenly dimmed the light, but it would always brighten again, and by the time they had finished their malteds, the clouds had all gone by. In the daylight, Sarah's short red hair gleamed like bright copper. She slurped the last of her drink through her straw and said, "Haven't seen much of Fergie lately."

Johnny shrugged, stirring the dregs of his malted with a straw. "He's been kind of depressed or something. I don't know what's wrong with him, except the weather."

"I think the rain got everybody down. Did your cellar fill up with water?"

Johnny shook his head. "Yours?"

Sarah laughed. "Man, did it ever! I thought my mom was going to have a kitten. She thought the whole place was going to, like, wash out to sea or something. Dad borrowed an electric pump from someplace and tried to empty it out. Dixon, you would have died laughing."

Johnny grinned. Sarah's dad was a red-haired, tall, thin, bespectacled English professor who was amiable but vague. He could tell you all about Shakespeare's sonnets or Nathaniel Hawthorne's short stories, but anything mechanical was beyond him. Johnny had once seen him try to open a door for ten minutes, only to discover that he was using the wrong key. "Didn't succeed, huh?"

With a grin, Sarah said, "Well, see, the pump has this long hose. Dad hooked everything up and put the hose into the kitchen sink. Then he tied a rope to the handle of the pump and lowered it into the cellar. The pump fired right up and began to shoot water out of the hose. Trouble is, Dad hadn't tied the hose down or anything, so it jumped out of the sink and glurped about fifty gallons of water onto the kitchen floor. So there was Dad standing halfway down the cellar steps, and the water he was pumping out was draining right back down through the cellar door and making a little waterfall right behind him, and he didn't notice until his shoes were full."

Johnny smiled. "But did he get it fixed finally?"

"Oh, finally. He says he's going to get some waterproofing gloop from the hardware store and fix the leaks. I'll let you know if he glues himself to the floor or anything."

"It could be worse," said Johnny. "Your dad could have asked Professor Childermass to help."

Sarah chuckled. Professor Roderick R. Childermass taught history at the same college where Sarah's dad taught English. The professor lived across Fillmore Street from Johnny and his grandparents, and he was a crabby, cranky old man whose explosive temper was a legend in Duston Heights. A short man with gold-rimmed eyeglasses, wild white muttonchop whiskers, and a red, pitted nose like a very ripe strawberry, Professor Childermass was no good with tools and repairs, even though he liked to think of himself as quite a handyman. His building projects usually resulted in his wrecking some part of his big old stucco house. After spending a few hours in his fuss closet—a specially soundproofed room where he could rant and rage and let off steam—the professor would call some real repairmen and then make their lives miserable until they had undone his damage. Oddly, even though Professor Childermass had the sociability of an angry porcupine, he was a good friend of Johnny's, and he liked Johnny's friends Sarah and Fergie too. The elderly man and the young friends got along well, even though most people in the small town would give Professor Childermass a very wide berth.

"Hey," Sarah said, straightening up in her chair. "There goes Fergie now."

She and Johnny hurried out of Peter's Sweet Shop. "Fergie!" yelled Johnny. "Wait up!"

A strange thing happened. Fergie jumped as if he had just been scared out of his wits. He looked over his shoulder at them, his face pale, and then he ducked into an alley. Sarah's expression looked just as puzzled as Johnny felt. "What's with him?" she asked.

"C'mon." Johnny and Sarah trotted to the alley, but Fergie was nowhere in sight. "He must've run off somewhere," said Johnny. "I wonder what's the matter with him."

"Who knows?" Sarah said. "Sometimes I think your friend Fergie is just a little weird, Dixon."

Soon after that, Sarah went home. Fergie's strange behavior still bothered Johnny, and he trudged to Fillmore Street sunk deep in thought. He dropped his schoolbooks off at his house, then went across the street to see Professor Childermass.

The professor was just taking some walnut brownies from his oven. He loved to bake gooey chocolate treats, and these smelled delicious. "We'll let them cool," said the professor, "until they are exactly the right temperature, not hot but wonderfully warm, and then we'll wade in and see what damage we can do. Now, John Michael, what do you have on your mind besides your hair? You look woebegone and befuddled."

Johnny pulled up a chair and sat at the professor's kitchen table. "It's Fergie," he said. "He's acting strange. Today he ran away from me for no reason at all."

"That does sound odd," agreed the professor. "Are you sure he was running away from you?"

With a shrug, Johnny explained what had happened. "He looked right at us," he finished. "He had to know it was Sarah and me. But he dived into the alley, and then he must have run away."

"Strange," said Professor Childermass. "But maybe Byron has something worrying him. You know, John, I have spells when I just have to be alone. So do you, for that matter. I suspect that Byron has some reason for behaving so peculiarly. He's your good friend, after all."

"I know. But if he's in trouble or something, I'd like to help him if I could."

The professor got up, cut the brownies, and poured two tall, foamy glasses of milk. "This is going to spoil your dinner," he warned. "So if you tell your grandmother I gave you this heavenly treat, I shall insist that you held me at gunpoint and forced it out of me." He set a saucer with a huge brownie in front of Johnny. Then he lifted his glass solemnly. "To our friend Byron. May his problems be over soon."

Johnny clinked his glass of milk against the professor's, and then he dug in. The brownie was indeed tasty, and Johnny could have eaten another, but Professor Childermass drew the line at one. "Your grandmother might eventually forgive me if you can bring yourself to eat a few bites of dinner," he pronounced. "If I let you gorge yourself so that you can only look at your peas and carrots with the expression of a sick puppy, she'll run me out of town." He took Johnny's saucer and glass and added them to a perilous stack of dirty dishes in the sink. "John, I tell you what. You go home and call Byron and ask him if he wants to see a movie tonight. I'll treat. Maybe if he goes with us, he'll break down and tell us what is going on. Anyway, it can't hurt to try."

Johnny agreed. As soon as he got home, he called Fergie, who answered in a wary voice. "Hi," said Johnny cheerfully. He had decided not to mention what had happened outside Peter's Sweet Shop. "Want to go to the movies tonight?"

"I dunno," Fergie said. "I have a lot of homework an' stuff."

Johnny laughed. "Fergie, it's Friday afternoon! You've got the whole weekend for homework." It was true. And both Fergie and Johnny always put off homework until the last possible minute.

"Well, all right," Fergie said at last.

Johnny picked up the Duston Heights newspaper that his grandfather had left on the dining room table. He leafed to the movie and comic-strip pages. "The show's at seven forty-five," he said. "So Professor Childermass and I will meet you at the theater at seven-thirty, okay?"

"Sure," Fergie said without much enthusiasm.

Johnny said good-bye and hung up. He could hear his grandmother bustling around the kitchen, preparing dinner, and he could smell a wonderful aroma of chicken, gravy, and pastry. Despite the malted he had drunk at Peter's Sweet Shop and the brownie and milk the professor had given him, Johnny's mouth watered. Gramma Dixon's chicken potpie was one of her best dishes, and she was a fabulous cook. He went into the kitchen and helped set the table. Grampa came downstairs from his nap, and they all had dinner together. A little after seven Johnny went over to the professor's house and the two of them strolled downtown.

"There he is," Johnny said in a low voice.

Fergie was leaning against the wall of the theater with his shoulders hunched and his hands in his pockets. He was wearing his motorcycle jacket, jeans, and boots, and looked like a young roughneck. As the professor and Johnny approached, Fergie looked up and gave them a sickly kind of smile.

"So, Byron," said Professor Childermass. "How is every little thing?"

"Fine," Fergie said shortly.

The professor stared at him hard through his gold-rimmed glasses. He waited, but Fergie added nothing else. Johnny bit his lip. Fergie was definitely acting strange. Usually he was a real smart aleck, the kind of kid who didn't hesitate to make a wisecrack to an adult. But the professor made no remark. He bought the tickets, and the three stocked up on popcorn and orange sodas before going into the auditorium.

The picture wasn't a very good one. It was a Western about a singing cowboy who was trying to run a gang of rustlers out of a frontier town, apparently by organizing a chorus of cowpokes to sing at the bad guys until they gave up. The professor snorted and made grumpy exclamations whenever something really dumb happened in the movie, and Johnny laughed in all the wrong places. Fergie just sat slouched in his seat, like a lump.

When the movie ended, Professor Childermass stood, stretched, and said, "Well, *that* was as fine a waste of three dollars as anything I have seen lately. Come along with us, Byron, and we'll finish off a plate of brownies. Then I'll drive you home."

They walked through the cool darkness. After minutes of silence, suddenly Fergie blurted out, "Professor, I gotta ask you something. Did you ever hear of a guy by the name of Jarmyn Thanatos?"

Professor Childermass stopped abruptly underneath a lamppost. The yellow light made highlights in his white hair and side-whiskers and cast deep shadows that hid his eyes. "Where in the world did you hear that name?" he demanded.

Fergie shrugged. "Aw, I read it in a book or somethin'. It's no big deal—"

"Come along." The professor strode off briskly, and both Johnny and Fergie had to trot to catch up to him. When Fergie tried to ask him about Jarmyn Thanatos again, the professor waved an impatient hand. "Later, Byron! I'll tell you everything I know about that wretched miscreant, but I will do it only in the comfort of my own little home."

When they reached the professor's house, he led them up to his cluttered second-floor study. As usual, blue-bound exam papers and essays all but hid his desktop, and more had fallen to the floor, forming little academic paper dunes. From its round stand near the desk, the professor's stuffed owl stared at them with wide eyes, its miniature Red Sox cap tilted at a jaunty angle. "Sit down," growled Professor Childermass. He settled into the chair behind his desk, and the two boys moved stacks of books from a couple of armchairs and sat facing him. "Now, first things first," said the professor. "Byron, where on earth did you come across the name Jarmyn Thanatos?"

Fergie looked uncomfortable. He twisted his feet back, hooking them around the short front legs of his armchair. "Well, I dunno. Like I started to say, it was just somethin' in a book. It's no big deal or anything."

"It is not a name you should concern yourself with," returned the professor sharply. "The late unlamented Mr. Thanatos is no business of yours."

Fergie's face got red. "Well, gee! Excuse me for breathing, Prof. I didn't mean to ruffle your feathers or anything. What's so bad about old Whosis, anyway?"

Professor Childermass drummed his fingers on the desk, then pushed up his glasses and rubbed his eyes. After he had readjusted his spectacles, he muttered, "I apologize, Byron. I was unreasonable."

Fergie mumbled something that Johnny couldn't quite hear. Johnny asked, "Is it a secret?"

With a sharp bark of a laugh, Professor Childermass said, "No secret, John. Just an embarrassing family skeleton, that's all. Now, let me see. You boys know all about such charlatans as Comte de Saint-Germain and Cagliostro, don't you?"

Johnny and Fergie exchanged a glance, and Fergie shrugged. "Yeah, I've read about 'em. They lived in France back in the eighteenth century and pretended to be wizards who had the secret of eternal life, right?"

"Close enough," answered the professor. "Well, Jarmyn Thanatos was their brother under the skin. He was active in Vermont, New Hampshire, and western Massachusetts late in the last century and made quite a name for himself—as a medicine-show quack, a con artist, and a miserable mountebank, that is. He claimed to have the secrets of the Hand of Glory, the philosopher's stone to turn lead into gold, and the universal elixir that cured every disease and disorder from athlete's foot to yaws. Anyone with half a brain could see the man was a catchpenny swindler—anyone but my dear father, that is."

The professor fell silent. Johnny licked his lips. "Professor, did Thanatos cheat your father or something?"

With a sigh, the old man said, "Give the man a cigar. Right you are, John. And not only my father—around 1885 or 1886, the scoundrel bilked thousands of dollars from a half dozen people in my hometown, all because he assured them that some harebrained scheme of his was a super-duper ironclad investment."

"What kind of scheme, Prof?" asked Fergie.

Frowning, Professor Childermass said, "Well . . . it was a scheme to discover the secret of eternal life. Old Jarmyn Thanatos convinced those people that if they trusted him, he would find a way to let them live forever!"

With a strangled cry, Fergie jumped up from his chair. He clapped his hands to his ears. The other two stared at him as if he had lost his mind. He had turned so pale that he looked as if he were about to faint. "Fergie?" asked Johnny. "What's the matter?"

Fergie dropped his hands and stammered, "D-didn't you h-hear that?"

"Hear what?" asked the professor in a quiet voice.

"The bell!" Fergie shouted. "That awful bell!" He looked from Johnny to the professor and back, and then he turned and ran out of the study. Johnny heard his friend's feet clattering on the stairs, and a moment later the front door slammed.

Professor Childermass cleared his throat. "Did *you* hear a bell, John?"

Johnny shook his head. "No."

"Nor did I. Because no bell rang."

"Professor?" said Johnny in a small voice. "What do you suppose happened to Fergie?"

Professor Childermass crossed his arms and scowled. "I don't know, John. Byron has either lost his mind— or else he's enjoying some kind of practical joke. Knowing our friend's warped sense of humor, I'd guess it was the latter."

But Johnny wasn't sure. He wasn't sure at all.

) 23 (

CHAPTER THREE

The next day was Saturday. When Fergie woke up that morning, he had the strange feeling that he had been having a horrible dream—but he couldn't remember anything about it. Except that it was bad. He had a confused impression that someone was yanking him this way and that, shaking him the way a terrier shakes a rat. But nothing else was clear. He got out of bed and slowly got dressed in a T-shirt and jeans.

His mom was sitting at the kitchen table, and she looked up from the morning newspaper when he came in. "Good morning," she said brightly. She was a worn-looking woman with stringy gray hair, and she was wearing an apron over a red flower-patterned dress. Years of pinching pennies and hard work had left her with a tired expression, but she always perked up when talking to

Fergie or his dad. Mrs. Ferguson put the paper aside and asked, "What do you want for breakfast today?"

"I dunno," mumbled Fergie. "What're you having, Mom?"

"Coffee and Cream of Wheat," she told him.

Fergie made a face. He hated all hot cereals and would just as soon eat a big pot of steaming library paste. He went to the refrigerator and got out a quart milk bottle. He rattled the cereal bowls, put one on the table, and then retrieved a box of cornflakes from the cabinet. He shook some of these into the bowl, spilling a few, and then sloshed milk over them. Some of it splashed out onto the table.

Mrs. Ferguson said, "Here, I'll get a towel—"

"Mom!" Fergie rolled his eyes. "For Pete's sake, you'd think I was a baby or somethin'." He got up and found a kitchen towel, which he used to swab up the spilled milk. Then he wolfed down his bowl of cereal. He dumped the empty bowl and the spoon into the sink. After breakfast Fergie hurried back upstairs to his room and locked the door. His heart was beating fast. The closet door had a frame that stuck out about an inch all the way around. Long ago he had rigged up a secret hiding place by taping a flap of cardboard across the top of the frame and to the inside wall of the closet. The cardboard made a sort of pocket that he could put private stuff in. The book he had taken from the public library was there now. He had meant to look at it long before this, but somehow he had never had the courage. Every time he had taken the book down, he remembered the loud, eerie bell—and the mysterious old man. Three times before, he had replaced the unopened book in his secret spot, but he promised himself that this morning he was actually going to read some of its pages.

Pushing a chair over to the open closet door, Fergie climbed up and reached inside, felt for the top of the cardboard pocket, and then fished the book out. It felt strangely heavy in his hands, as if it were bound in sheets of lead instead of cardboard and cloth. He got off the chair, sprawled on his bed, and turned the book this way and that, just studying it.

In the light of morning, it didn't look frightening at all. The black cloth cover was fine grained and might once have looked expensive and neat. Now, though, the corners were battered and smashed, with frayed threads and the gray cardboard showing. The spine was cracked along its length, and the pages didn't quite meet smoothly in the center. The stamped red title-and-author label looked as if it had been a shiny metallic color, but now it was a dusty crimson, with tiny flakes missing here and there.

"*The Book of True Wishes*," muttered Fergie. "Yeah. Like fun it is." He was a sensible boy who always looked for the logical and rational explanation of anything odd. He didn't believe for a moment in genies' lamps or wishing rings, and he knew there was no such thing as a fairy godmother who made your dreams come true. Still, he had to admit that the book gave him a very unusual feeling. A feeling of, well, power, as if he knew something that no one else on earth even suspected.

Fergie clenched his teeth and opened the book.

Bo-o-o-n-nng! The windows of his room actually vibrated as the heavy bell tolled. Fergie caught his breath and waited for his mother to come rushing up the stairs to ask what in the world he was doing. But nothing happened.

He looked down and frowned. He had meant to open the book to the first page, but the thin leaves had stuck together, and he had cracked the volume to two full pages. He tried to turn back, but the left page seemed stuck to the cover. With a grunt, Fergie read the incomplete first paragraph:

> warnings, you must freely choose to read. That is
> an easy choice, my boy, for you are always eager
> for knowledge. And the knowledge you gain from
> this book will never leave you. Like the book itself,
> it cannot be destroyed.

"Oh, man," said Fergie, shaking his head. This was too much. He knew that it would be easy to destroy this little volume—it was only a thin book about six by nine inches. It could be burned or ground to a pulp or the pages could just be ripped out and scattered. It—

Fergie paused, feeling a chill creep up his spine. His eye had gone to the next sentence in the book: "Of course, you're thinking the book can be burned or ground to a pulp. Or maybe the pages could just be ripped out and scattered. But you are wrong. You may try now."

"Okay," said Fergie, feeling suddenly angry. He

grasped the right sheet and tore it—or tried to tear it.

To Fergie's astonishment, he could neither rip the page nor pull it out of the book. The paper felt flimsy and thin, so smooth that it was almost oily, but it was too sturdy for him to injure it in any way. And he had the sick feeling that even if he threw it on a blazing fire, the book wouldn't be scorched. When he let go of the page, it turned itself. The reverse side of that sheet was blank, and the right page held only five words, in big black letters:

What Is Your First Wish?

"Huh," snorted Fergie. "Okay, Mr. Whosis, I'll play along. I wish my dad had a job that paid him so good he didn't have to travel. What about that?"

He turned the page. And blinked. He felt his heart trying to climb up his throat and jump out his mouth. There was his own father's name—and his. Swallowing hard, Fergie frantically began to read:

> Mr. Ferguson hardly suspected that when he had trouble with his automobile on his way back to Duston Heights he would ask help from a passerby who owned a thriving business. When he began to speak to the stranger, he had no way of knowing that the prosperous fellow would offer him a good

job before their talk was through. And when he accepted the job offer, Mr. Ferguson could only look ahead with eager anticipation to the pleasure his announcement would give to his wife, Alice, and to their son, Byron. They would be so happy, and he would not have to travel ever again!

And Fergie would be secretly proud that he had given his father the opportunity. He would not even mind the small price that he had to pay.

Bo-o-o-n-nng!

The thunderous peal of the bell made Fergie jump and yelp. The book fell closed, and he leaped out of bed, shoved the chair over to the closet, and stuck the mysterious volume back in his hiding place. He slammed the closet door shut and went running downstairs. He reached the kitchen doorway and froze, holding onto the door frame. His mother stood at the sink, washing the breakfast dishes, and she looked around in alarm. "What's wrong?" she asked with a gasp.

"Uh—did you hear somethin' just now?" panted Fergie.

"I heard you running downstairs like a herd of rhinos," his mother replied, drying her hands on a white dish towel.

"When—when's Dad comin' home?" asked Fergie.

Mrs. Ferguson frowned at her son. "Why? You know he won't be back until next Friday afternoon," she said. "He still has all of his New Hampshire territory to visit."

Fergie tried to keep his voice steady. "Have—have

you heard from him? I mean, in the last coupla days?"

"He called me last night from Burlington," said Mrs. Ferguson.

"An'—an' he was all right and everything? Did he, uh, say anything about his job or—or anything?" finished Fergie lamely.

Looking worried, Mrs. Ferguson shook her head. "No, dear. He just said he was looking forward to coming home again."

Fergie closed his eyes and pictured the family's car, an old blue Ford. Then he asked one more question: "Did he say anything about the car actin' up?"

"No, son," said his mother. "Are you sure you're all right? You look a little feverish."

"Mom, I'm fine, okay?" Fergie took a long, shaky breath. *The Book of True Wishes*, huh? Well, it sure didn't seem to be doing its job! So much for magic and sorcery and all that baby stuff! Fergie turned in the doorway and stalked toward the front door. "I'm goin' out," he said.

"Where are you going?" his mom asked.

"Out," Fergie yelled over his shoulder. He got his leather jacket from the hall closet and shrugged into it.

Mrs. Ferguson followed him into the hall. "But Byron, when will you—"

"I'll be back when I get back!" snapped Fergie. He banged out the door. Something made him look over his shoulder. His mom stood in the doorway, her hands clasped in front of her apron, an expression of distress on her face. Fergie almost waved at her in a reassuring way. But then he heard, or imagined he heard, a voice:

"Don't bother with her. You've got big things ahead of you."

And so he hunched into his jacket, lowered his head, and went trotting off into a warm spring morning, heading for the athletic field. He was glad to get away from home, he told himself. He was really looking forward to playing flies and grounders with Johnny and Sarah. That would get his mind off that loopy book, off the strange man in the library, and off his mother, who lately had developed a real knack for getting on his nerves. Still, when Fergie thought about how worried his mother had looked, his stomach seemed to fall.

And so he decided not to think about her anymore. Maybe never again, in fact.

CHAPTER FOUR

The rest of the weekend passed quietly. The next week began with warm, sunny skies, and the people of Duston Heights began to think that spring had arrived at last, but the balmy weather did not improve Johnny's spirits. He and Sarah had played a few rounds of flies and grounders with Fergie on Saturday. Fergie wasn't his usual cheerful self, but glum and gruff. He had left their game early, and they hadn't seen him again. Then the weekend was over, and school was back in session and Johnny got busy studying for a big Latin test.

But he didn't stop thinking about his friend, and he and Sarah talked the matter over. On Wednesday after they left school, Sarah suggested that they head over to Haggstrum College, where both Professor Childermass and Sarah's dad taught. She thought they might be able to find something about Mr. Jarmyn Thanatos in the college library. As the dependent of a faculty member, she had a library card, and the college library staff seemed to know her well.

She and Johnny went through the card catalogue without finding any books by or about Mr. Thanatos. Then Sarah had a bright idea. The Duston Heights newspaper, the *Gazette*, dated all the way back to before the Civil War, and the college library had shelves of huge oversized volumes of the bound newspaper. Fortunately, the Duston Heights Historical Society had created a set of indexes for the newspapers, and Sarah suggested that she and Johnny tackle these.

They had to go down into the basement. It was creepy there, with long pine tables scuffed and scarred by generations of students, tall gloomy shelves, and scattered lightbulbs in white metal shades throwing little yellow islands of illumination. The *Gazette* indexes alone filled most of one shelf, and they hauled a batch of these over to one of the tables, beginning with the index for 1884. They looked for the name Thanatos in each one, and they also checked for the name Childermass, although the professor's father had been on the faculty of Princeton University.

For a long time they had no luck at all. Finally, Sarah grunted in satisfaction and said, "Here's something, Dixon. Says here that the 1886 papers have three stories about someone named Thanatos. May 10, October 27, and November 14. Let's get them."

The old newspapers were bound in crinkly maroon

covers held together by silvery rivets. Their spines bore a library call number and the months and year of the newspapers each oversized book contained. Two heavy volumes covered 1886, and Johnny pulled both out, releasing a cloud of dust that smelled old and dry and stale. He sniffled and carried the heavy volumes over to the table, where he plumped them down under a light.

Sarah opened the first one. The newspapers inside were fragile, brown and brittle with age, and she had to turn each page carefully to keep it from flaking away. The *Gazette* had been published on Mondays, Wednesdays, Fridays, and Sundays in 1886, and most of the issues had eight pages. These were densely packed with type, and there were no photos or drawings at all—just column after column of old newsprint, with the stories separated by thick black lines. They found the issue for May 10 that the index had listed, and skimmed through all the columns. The story was a small one, on page four. Its headline read, "Mystery in Ellisboro."

Johnny read through the article. It said that an eleven-year-old boy named Tommy McCorkle, the shy and bookish son of a wealthy banker in the town of Ellisboro, Vermont, had disappeared on Monday, May 3. The town constables had searched everywhere for the boy, and they had questioned one J. Thanatos, who lived in an old house on the edge of town. Someone thought that he had seen Mr. Thanatos talking to Tommy on the afternoon of the third, but Mr. Thanatos had proved that he was elsewhere at the time.

"This doesn't tell us much," Johnny complained. "We don't even know if it's the same person."

Sarah rolled her eyes. "C'mon, Dixon. How many J. Thanatoses can there *be*? It's not a name like John Smith, you know!"

"Okay, okay," said Johnny. "What's the next story?"

The next one was from October 27. Its headline read, "Mystery of Missing Boy Deepens." Johnny frowned. A frightened boy had told an Ellisboro constable that he had seen the face of his friend Tommy McCorkle looking out of a second-floor window of Jarmyn Thanatos's house. When officials investigated, they found the place completely locked up and apparently deserted. After getting a warrant, the constables broke into the old house and searched it thoroughly, but they could find no trace of the missing boy—or of the mysterious Mr. Thanatos.

"Okay," grunted Johnny. "I have to admit, this is the right guy. Next?"

The next article was the last one, and it was the most puzzling of all. It was on the front page of the November 14 issue, under the headline "Search for Missing Tommy McCorkle Yields Mysterious Orphan." The article was a long one. Johnny read it, and then he took a deep breath. "What's it say?" demanded Sarah, reaching to tug the bound volume around.

"Don't bother," said Johnny. "I'll tell you. The police started looking for Mr. Thanatos, but they couldn't find any trace of him. And then they got a letter from the Hannah Duston Orphanage, right here in town."

"I never heard of an orphanage here," objected Sarah.

Johnny shrugged impatiently. "It's probably not here anymore. I mean, this was about seventy years ago. Anyhow, the director of the orphanage read in the paper about the search for Tommy McCorkle and about Mr. Thanatos, and when a strange kid showed up on the doorstep of the place, she seemed to think it might be the McCorkle boy. So she telegraphed the Ellisboro police, and Banker McCorkle and Constable Padgett rode down on the train. But they were disappointed, because the kid wasn't Tommy at all. He was the same age as Tommy, but he said he was Adam Nemo, the nephew of Jarmyn Thanatos. And the funny thing was that a letter came the next day from a bank in Duston Heights. It said that Jarmyn Thanatos had opened a substantial savings account for his nephew, and that the boy was not to be adopted out. When he turned eighteen, he was to get all the money in the account. Meanwhile, a check went to the orphanage to pay for his room and board until he could claim the money. But the strangest thing was that when he did turn eighteen—his birthday happened to be October 31—Adam Nemo had to change his name before he could claim the money."

"Change his name to what?" asked Sarah.

Johnny stared at her. "To Jarmyn Thanatos," he said in a whisper.

Sarah shivered. "That's *weird*," she said.

They read through more indexes, but they could find no further mention of any Jarmyn Thanatos. Sarah checked for stories about the Hannah Duston Orphanage, though, and she found a very odd one in the 1890's. They looked it up. It was the story of how the Hannah Duston Orphanage had burned to the ground on the night of October 31, 1893. No lives were lost, but the whole structure went up in flames, and all the records that had been stored in the basement were completely burned.

Sarah counted under her breath: "Eighty-six, eighty-seven, eighty-eight—"

"What are you doing?" asked Johnny.

She shook her head and continued counting until she reached ninety-three. Then she stared at Johnny. "Adam Nemo would have had his eighteenth birthday on October 31, 1893," she said. "And then if he wanted to inherit his money, he became Jarmyn Thanatos."

The name hung in the air between them. Johnny had an attack of goose pimples. He felt as if he were suffocating down there in the dark, stuffy basement. He and Sarah hurried upstairs and out into the warm afternoon sunlight. "What do we do now?" asked Sarah.

Johnny shook his head. "I don't know. But I think we'd better tell the professor. This is all getting too mysterious, if you ask me."

"I think you're right," agreed Sarah.

They hurried away. Neither of them noticed that someone watched them go. It was a short, thin, elderly man with long white hair spreading over his shoulders. He smiled grimly to himself and then went into the library. He stayed for only a few minutes before coming out again. This time when he walked, something rustled in his coat pockets. The sound was whispery and soft, like crumpled sheets of old newspaper.

That night Fergie had a hard time getting to sleep. He tossed and turned for a long time. He tried counting sheep, but that didn't work. He had an old, beat-up Motorola radio beside his bed and he turned it on with the sound very low. He twiddled the dial until he found a station playing some boring music, and he lay and listened to that for a while. None of it seemed to help. He wanted to get out of bed, climb up in the chair, and pull *The Book of True Wishes* from its hiding place. But with another part of his mind, a stubborn one, he refused to do it. He would wait and see. If his dad came back home on Friday and nothing unusual had happened, then he would toss the book away. And if the crazy things the book said turned out to be true . . . well, he would think about that later.

It was past midnight when Fergie finally dozed off. Soon he was sleeping deeply, and then he started to have a strange dream. It was the kind of dream he had experienced only a couple of times before, one in which he knew he was dreaming. Yet at the same time everything seemed so real. . . .

Fergie was walking along a sidewalk in a little town somewhere. The street he was on was full of small white cottages, each with a neat green front yard and a white picket fence. The sidewalk was made of wood, not cement, and the street was unpaved. For some reason things that were a few feet away from Fergie looked blurred and unclear, while objects in the distance were sharp and crisp. He could see humped green mountains far off beyond the vague shapes of buildings. It was silent. No voices called out. No leaf rustled in the wind. All was as still as death.

Then from behind him came an odd, raspy, metallic noise. Fergie looked around and blinked. A young kid was running down the street toward him. In front of the boy rolled an iron hoop, the kind that used to go around the huge barrels called hogsheads. The running figure held a short T-shaped stick, and with this he kept the hoop rolling.

But the oddest thing was the way the boy was dressed. He was wearing a blue middy blouse, short pants, and black leather shoes. And his hair was long, curling down over his ears. He reminded Fergie of the picture of Buster Brown that he had seen in shoe stores. "Hey," Fergie yelled.

The boy paid no attention and rolled his hoop right past. A horse-drawn wagon came clopping along in the other direction. The old gray spotted horse seemed to be doing all the work, because the driver slumped in his seat, chin on chest, asleep.

"This is a crazy dream," muttered Fergie. Usually his dreams were far more exciting, filled with adventures and chases and pirate fights. He walked along for a while and found himself in the center of a small town. A green park was before him. On the four streets facing the park stood businesses, some with horses tied to hitching posts in front of them. A few people were walking on the wooden sidewalks, all of them dressed in old-fashioned clothing. Fergie spoke to many of them, but none gave the least sign of having heard him.

The dream dragged on and on. Fergie began to feel nervous. He was like a ghost in this strange world of living shadows. People couldn't see or hear him, and when he tried to touch them, he couldn't. He was always farther away than he thought, or the person made a sudden movement that just eluded him. Inside a dry-goods store, where spools of thread, thimbles, and needles lay on a counter, he tried to pick up something, but everything was impossible to move. It was as if the things had been cemented to the counter. But then a woman in an old-fashioned dress came over and picked up a packet of needles that Fergie had been unable to budge. He got red in the face and yelled at the woman. She turned away. Obviously, she had not even heard him.

Fergie rushed back into the street. He screamed and leaped. He capered and howled. No one paid him the least attention. By that time Fergie was sweating. This dream had gone on far too long. What if he never woke up? Or what if he were dead, and Catholics were right? This might be purgatory, where he would have to spend thousands of years alone, invisible, an outcast. He might never see Johnny or the professor again, or his mother and father—

Fergie ran through the streets like a crazy person. He did not watch where he was going, and he did not care. More than he had ever wanted anything in his whole life, he wanted to wake up. He ran until he could hardly lift his feet, until his breath burned his lungs. Finally, fatigued, he slowed. He plodded along, not wanting to halt. He had the creepy feeling that something was stalking him. Some lines from Samuel Taylor Coleridge's spooky poem "The Rime of the Ancient Mariner" ran through his mind:

> Like one that on a lonesome road
> Doth walk in fear and dread,
> And having once turned round walks on,
> And turns no more his head;
> Because he knows a frightful fiend
> Doth close behind him tread.

But at last, exhausted, Fergie stumbled to a stop. And then he saw that he had fled right out of the town. He stood on a hill overlooking the village, a little clump of white houses and buildings gleaming in the sun. He was on a dirt road. And as he stared down into the valley, suddenly, from everywhere at once, came the terrible loud pealing of a great bell, so close that it hurt his ears.

"I gotta wake up," groaned Fergie. He turned this way and that, looking for any way to escape this deadly dream.

And then he saw the house. It was behind a grove of trees, some distance away from the road. He could see the upper stories only, and he could see that attached to the house was a bell tower. Somehow he knew that was where the terrible sound was coming from. He had to stop it.

He turned off the road, down a weedy, overgrown

driveway. The ground was rutted and treacherous, and round, smooth stones stuck up to trip him. He pushed through brush and finally came out in front of the old house. The bell tower was on the right, attached to the side of the house, but it had its own door. As Fergie came close, the door slowly opened, as if its hinges were rusty. Another peal of the bell made Fergie's ears ache, but he staggered forward and into the yawning black doorway.

A stairway ran up the sides of the tower. Fergie began to climb it, grasping the rail, which felt spongy and slimy beneath his hand. When he was halfway up, the bell tolled again, and the whole structure vibrated as if it were about to cave in. Fergie ground his teeth. His eyes were watering. He climbed up, up, up, until he stood on a platform with the bell only a yard away. To his despair, he saw that the bell had no rope or clapper—and yet *something* had produced that horrible sound. "I gotta climb down," Fergie muttered. "It'd kill me if that thing rang with me right beside it."

He turned—and stood as though frozen.

Below him, something was floating up the stairway. It was round and white, and it was a face. The face of a boy about his age or a little younger. But the mouth writhed in agony, and the eyes held a tormented look. The figure came closer, and Fergie could see that it was a ghost. It floated a few feet above the stairway, its feet not even moving. It stretched out its hands toward Fergie in an imploring way.

"Set me free!" said the apparition. "He locked me in a coffin!"

Fergie backed away. He stood in an arch in the belfry, with thin air at his back. "Leave me alone!" he shouted.

"Don't make the wish!" moaned the ghost. "Don't let him trap you!"

The bell did not move an inch, and yet it tolled, and the sound struck Fergie like a physical blow. He toppled backward, his hands scrabbling for a hold. Fergie felt himself falling to the ground, fifty feet below. He tumbled through the air, seeing the belfry rush away above him, the ground rush up to meet him—

"*No!*"

Trembling, Fergie sat up in bed. He gasped for breath. Then he realized that he had awakened from the dream.

Just then an announcer's voice came from the radio: "And now we sign off until 7:00 A.M. tomorrow. Good night, and sleep tight, out there in radio land."

Then Fergie jumped out of bed as if he had been scalded. For from the radio came three evenly spaced tolls of a great bell.

CHAPTER FIVE

The next Saturday morning was bright and sunny. Johnny woke up early and climbed onto his bike. The town was still mostly asleep when he pedaled through— an old milk truck was making deliveries, and he saw a paperboy tossing copies of the morning paper up onto people's steps and porch roofs. But no businesses were open.

Johnny crossed the bridge over the Merrimack River and rode into the part of town called Cranbrook. He turned in at the little two-story house owned by the Ferguson family. Fergie's dad was home from his sales trip, because his rusty old blue Ford was parked in the drive-way. Swinging off his bike, Johnny kicked down the stand and stood the Schwinn under the shade of an oak.

He went up onto Fergie's front steps and settled down to wait. One way or another, Johnny was going to see Fergie this morning.

He waited more than half an hour. Then he heard noises coming from inside the house, the rattle of dishes and the scraping of chairs around the breakfast table. Taking a deep breath, Johnny got up and knocked on the front door. He heard footsteps, and then the door swung open. Mrs. Ferguson stood there, looking a little startled. "Oh—Johnny," she said. "I couldn't imagine who was knocking on our door this early. Come in and have some breakfast."

"Thanks, Mrs. Ferguson," mumbled Johnny. She led him back to the kitchen, where Fergie and his dad were sitting at the breakfast table. They looked up in some surprise. "Hi," said Johnny to Fergie as he slipped into a chair.

"Hi," muttered Fergie, his face getting red. He looked sleepy and grouchy, as he usually did in the morning.

Mrs. Ferguson put a plate in front of Johnny. "Here," she said. "Have some eggs, Johnny? Some sausage? I'll put in two more pieces of toast for you."

"Thanks," said Johnny. She poured him a glass of orange juice, and Johnny tucked in. The scrambled eggs were delicious, fluffy and light, with Cheddar cheese whipped into them.

Mr. Ferguson smiled at him. "Well, I'm glad you're here, Johnny," he said. "Fergie and you are about as close as brothers, so I want you to hear my announcement too. Everybody, you will be glad to know that Mr. George Ferguson is moving up in the world. Beginning two weeks from Monday, I'm going to be a full-time salesman for Baxter Motors, right here in Duston Heights."

Mrs. Ferguson smiled at her husband. Johnny grinned and congratulated him. But Fergie just stared for a long time. "What?" he asked at last.

"It's true," said Mr. Ferguson proudly. "I'll have a salary, and I'll work on commission too, so I'll earn even more than my basic pay whenever I sell a used car. Funny thing—I was coming back home yesterday afternoon, and my car conked out just north of Ellisboro. Just died on me. So I pulled off onto the shoulder, and then this guy in a station wagon stopped to help. Turned out to be Mr. Bill Baxter, and while we tinkered with the car, we talked. We got her running again, Mr. Baxter wiped his hands on an old towel he had in the car, shook my hand, and offered me a job! What do you think of that, hey?"

Johnny stared at Fergie. His friend's face had turned white, as if with shock, and he shivered the way some people do when they say a goose has walked over their grave. But Fergie took a long drink of juice and finally said, "That's great, Dad."

Mr. Ferguson beamed at his son. "From now on I can be home a lot more," he said. "And we'll finally have enough money to replace the old stove and start a savings account for you so you can build up some money for college, Son."

Frowning, Johnny asked, "Did you say that your car broke down near Ellisboro, Mr. Ferguson?"

"Hm? Yes, and it was a good thing for me that Mr. Baxter came along, because Ellisboro is just a wide place in the road. I doubt if it even has a regular garage!"

Johnny cleared his throat. "Uh, that's up in Vermont, isn't it?"

"That's right," said Mr. Ferguson.

Johnny didn't say anything else. After breakfast, he asked Fergie, "Hey, you want to ride out to the park and play flies and grounders or something?"

Fergie shrugged. "I dunno, John baby. I don't really feel like runnin' after a dumb baseball."

"Well, let's just ride for a while."

Fergie went outside and climbed onto his beat-up old bike. The two friends rode back across the river and cruised along beside it, past the huge old brick mills, most of them long abandoned. "Hey, that was great news your dad told us," Johnny said after a while.

"Yeah," grunted Fergie.

Johnny looked over to his right. Fergie was pumping along, head down, as if he had to be somewhere and was late. "Uh, Fergie, is something wrong?" asked Johnny.

Fergie glared at him. "What's your problem, Dixon?"

His tone surprised Johnny. "Nothing. Only you've hardly talked to me at all this week. That's not like you."

"Well, nothin's wrong, so lay off," growled Fergie. "I'm just fine. Everything's fine."

"You know," said Johnny, trying to change the subject, "I read something funny about that little town where your dad's car broke down. Ellisboro, wasn't it? You know that name you asked Professor Childermass about, that Jarmyn Thanatos—"

"Leave me alone!" shouted Fergie. He wheeled his bike and headed back, whizzing along the cracked street.

Surprised, Johnny slowed and turned and tried to follow him. No use. Fergie was too far ahead and was much stronger than Johnny, so he easily outdistanced his friend. Johnny turned onto Fergie's street just in time to see Fergie hop off his bike, letting it crash to the ground. Fergie leaped up the steps and disappeared inside the house. The door slammed.

With his heart sinking, Johnny rode back to Fillmore Street. It seemed to him as though he had lost one of his oldest friends.

Fergie pounded up the stairs to his room. He closed the door behind him and threw himself onto his bed, clenching his fists. What was Dixon trying to do, asking him about Jarmyn Thanatos and shooting his mouth off about Mr. Ferguson's new job? It wasn't fair! Johnny's dad was special—a fighter pilot who had been shot down behind enemy lines in the Korean War. After his daring escape to an American base, he had even been featured in an issue of *Life* magazine. Why should Dixon care if Fergie's dad had a decent job at last? It wasn't any of his concern!

And for that matter, what right did Professor Childermass have, to stick his big, fat red nose in Fergie's business? They were hypocrites, all of them, that was it. Oh, they pretended to like you and be your friend, but behind your back they were always making fun of you, or thinking up ways of cutting you down. Well, he was through with all that! If the book could make one wish come true, it could make another, and another, and by the time he was finished—

Fergie sat up in bed, his throat dry. What had the book said about there being a price for his wishes? Was the price losing all his friends? He got up and shoved the chair over to the closet. He took the book down and began to leaf through from the front, but he couldn't find the page with the words about his father on it. In fact, as he frantically turned the thin opaque pages, he couldn't read any of the writing. Strange figures covered the pages, squiggly foreign letters like Arabic or Russian or something.

"I gotta find out about the payment," muttered Fergie. And when he turned the next page, suddenly he could read again.

Congratulations on your father's new job, Mr. Ferguson. You are the hero of the family! And they don't even suspect.

Now you are wondering about what payment will be demanded for your wish. It will not be anything you will not be glad to give. It is very simple. You must promise yourself that you will be a good student—and this is the book you must study.

"Okay," said Fergie. "Sure. Why not?" And he turned the page.

"And then he just tore off for home," said Johnny. "I tried to catch up, but he had a big lead."

"It's most odd," murmured Professor Childermass, frowning. He and Johnny were sitting in the professor's study, and Johnny had just blurted out the story of what had happened. "And you actually found a mention of that rapscallion Jarmyn Thanatos in the old newspapers?"

"Three of them," said Johnny. "And they all tied him in to that little town in Vermont where Mr. Ferguson's car broke down. The last one said that Mr. Thanatos's nephew was raised in the Hannah Duston Orphanage, right here in Duston Heights."

Professor Childermass pushed his spectacles up and rubbed his eyes. "That old place burned down about the time I was born," he muttered. "It used to be north of town, on Plaistow Road, I think." He pulled his spectacles down and glared. "And of course when it burned, all of its records were conveniently destroyed."

"Sarah said the same thing."

Nodding, Professor Childermass said, "Sarah is a very sharp young lady, John. Well, I hardly know what to do next. However, one course of action suggests itself. I believe I will telephone my old friend Charley Coote and ask him about the history of that miserable mountebank, Thanatos. There is a chance that he was something more than just a snake-oil peddler. He might have been up to something truly evil. And if he was, I want to know about it—forewarned is forearmed, you know." The old man rose from his chair and went to the hall, where the telephone was. For some minutes Johnny heard the rumble of the professor's voice, although he could not tell what the old man was saying to Dr. Coote. Then Professor Childermass returned with a puzzled expression. "Well, John, *something* is rotten in Denmark. Charley says he doesn't know very much about the story, but he does want to show me something—and he sounded pretty upset about whatever it is. I told Charley I'd drive up this afternoon."

"Can I go with you, Professor?" asked Johnny.

With a grim smile, the professor said, "Of course, John. You and I have been through too much together for us to have any secrets between us. I'll go ask your grandparents, and then we'll set off. We'll stop on the way for lunch."

Henry and Kate Dixon were happy to give their permission for the trip. Neither of them had been able to go to college, but they hoped that Johnny would attend some great university and become a world-renowned archaeologist. Both Professor Childermass and Dr. Charles Coote were scholars and university teachers who were a good influence on him.

Johnny sat in the front passenger seat as the professor drove his old maroon Pontiac north on Highway 125, into New Hampshire. Professor Childermass was not the best driver in the world, and occasionally Johnny grabbed the armrest and held on hard as they went careening around a slow truck or car. They stopped in a tiny little crossroads south of Durham because the professor had spotted a diner with a big green-and-white sign on the roof: Sam's Steak House. "These places usually serve a good burger," pronounced the professor as he parked the car.

The burgers were medium-well done, juicy, and delicious, piled high with tomatoes, lettuce, crisp dill pickles, and cheese, and they were served with thick French-fried potatoes. The professor drank a couple of cups of coffee with his lunch, and Johnny had a Coke. When they finished, the professor dropped a nickel into the slot of the pay phone and dialed his friend's number. Dr. Coote was already anxious because they were a little late, and Johnny and the professor drove from the diner straight to his old gray two-storied Victorian home on Pierce Street, a peaceful, quiet residential street in Durham.

A tall, reedy man with fluffy white hair and a long, bent nose that supported heavy horn-rimmed spectacles stood in the door waiting for them. He was Dr. Charles Coote, a specialist in the folklore of magic who taught at the University of New Hampshire in Durham. Even on his day off, he wore a tweedy gray jacket, a pale blue shirt, and a dark blue tie with tiny white luna moths on it. He ushered his guests inside, and they sat in his living room as Professor Childermass explained their interest in a man named Jarmyn Thanatos. When he finished, Dr. Coote leaned back in his armchair and made a steeple of his fingertips. "Now, that is an odd name," he murmured.

"Of course it is," growled Professor Childermass. "And an obvious alias! Why, the charlatan might as well have called himself 'Doctor Death' or 'Professor Doomsday' and made it plain to the dimmest dimwit in the crowd."

Johnny groaned. "I should have caught that," he said. "We studied William Cullen Bryant's poem 'Thanatopsis' in English last term, and the teacher told us the title meant *contemplation of death*. 'Thanatos' means *death*, doesn't it?"

"Bingo," said the professor, lighting one of his smelly black-and-gold Balkan Sobranie cigarettes. "And under that *nom de guerre*, the rascal cheated my father, along with about a hundred other people throughout New England, or so the story went. He must have made himself a rich man."

"Well, nothing specific comes to mind," said Dr. Coote nervously. "That is, I don't recall reading anything about any *Jarmyn* Thanatos, although I know something rather disturbing about *a* Thanatos, but I can certainly check out the name. You say he was active in Vermont, Roderick?"

"Ellisboro, according to what John discovered. And he seems to have been most prominent in the middle 1880's," returned the professor, blowing a blue cloud of smoke.

Dr. Coote looked faintly distressed as he waved the

smoke away. "Um, yes, I know the place. One of those scenic little villages that hasn't changed much in a hundred years or so, tucked into a valley in the Green Mountains."

"Where the mountain brooks sing lullabies to the nodding jonquils as they dream beside the limpid streams," snarled Professor Childermass in a sarcastic tone. "Charley, we don't need a travelogue. We just want to see what you can dig up on this Thanatos—especially if it has anything to do with magic."

"Oh, dear," murmured Dr. Coote. He stared at his visitors owlishly. "I suppose I should have expected that, with you two involved." He sighed. "Very well. I will do my best. But now let me show you the very unpleasant relic that came my way twenty-five years ago. I had forgotten all about it until you called with your questions. It's what I think you ought to see before proceeding any further with this business." He rose from his chair, swaying a little like a praying mantis, all elbows and knees, and went upstairs. Soon he brought back a wooden box about four inches square and three inches deep. "Well, here it is," Dr. Coote said.

"What's that?" asked Professor Childermass.

Dr. Coote carefully placed the box on the coffee table. "Look at the label," he said.

Johnny craned forward. A dry, yellowed label had been pasted to the box lid. Written on it in ink that had faded to a dull brown was the strange inscription *THANATOS MOUSE*. Johnny heard Professor Childermass gasp.

With a shaking hand, Dr. Coote prepared to open the

box. "This was dropped off at the university some twenty-five years ago as a curiosity," he said. "No one knew what to do with it, and eventually it came to me. I've had this box on a shelf in a closet for years and years, and it hasn't been opened since before the war." He lifted the lid and turned the box over. Something grayish-white rolled out.

Johnny blinked. The round object was a dead white mouse. Its ears were shriveled, its fur plastered down to its shrunken body, its tail a brittle-looking curl. The ribs showed through the skin, the lips had pulled far back from nasty yellowed teeth, and the ruby-red eyes had become sunken pits the color of scabs. "It's—it's a mouse mummy," he said thoughtfully.

Dr. Coote produced a pair of sugar tongs and gingerly rolled the creature over onto its belly. "I—I don't know if it will—do anything, but—just watch."

In an unsteady voice, Professor Childermass began, "Now, look here, Charley—"

"Professor!" yelled Johnny. "It's *moving*!"

Johnny felt the hair on his arms and the back of his neck prickle. The horrible little mummy was creeping forward slowly, its head creaking from side to side. From its mouth came a terrible jittery clicking sound, like a finger slowly run down the teeth of a comb. The dry claws scraped the table, the wizened nose twitched.

"You see?" asked Dr. Coote in a sick voice. He reached forward to pick up the creature with the sugar tongs.

It leaped! It jumped off the table—and right into

Johnny's lap! With a screech, Johnny lunged up from his chair, frantically swatting at the awful creature. It fell to the floor—and broke, just like a fragile cup. It shattered into three pieces, the head, the chest and front legs, and the hindquarters.

Dr. Coote looked down on the remains. "It's just as well," he said slowly. "Someone should have destroyed the wretched creature years ago. Gentlemen, that is, or was, the Thanatos mouse. I don't know anything about its origins—"

"D-Dr. Coote!" Johnny stammered. "Look at it—*it's still alive!*"

The pieces of the shattered mouse were still moving feebly. The mouth opened and shut. The front legs tried to drag themselves across the floor. The back legs twitched. With a grunt of disgust, Professor Childermass stamped on the thing, and when he lifted his foot, the three pieces had been ground to powder and loose strands of white hair. Horribly, they kept stirring even then. The professor strode to the fireplace, got the ash shovel and a whisk broom, and swept up the powder. "Charley," he said, "do we bury this or keep it for observation?"

"Oh, dear," said Dr. Coote. "Bury it. By all means, bury it." The three went into the backyard, where they dug a hole much deeper than seemed to be necessary, and they covered the dust over and packed down the dirt. When they had finished, Dr. Coote said, "Roderick, could *this* be connected to your Jarmyn Thanatos?"

"I think it is," growled the professor. "But I'd rather

not go into that right now, if you don't mind. Ugh! That creature is going to show up in my nightmares!"

"Very well, I won't press you," said Dr. Coote. "But do me a favor, please. If you find there's really some diabolical magic going on here, if Thanatos or his nephew is some kind of wicked sorcerer, I would greatly appreciate it if you would make your plans without me. I've had enough excitement already to last me a lifetime, my nerves aren't really very good, and you know I have weak legs—"

"Charley," said the professor grimly, "you just find out what you can, and leave all the rest to me."

"To us," said Johnny in a small voice. After all, Fergie was his friend. And if Fergie was in trouble, Johnny knew he had to help him get out of it.

If, that is, there were any way of helping him—any way at all.

CHAPTER SIX

Weeks went by. March turned into a drizzly, cool April, and April wore on toward May. Johnny and Sarah, who were in the same grade at St. Michael's School, studied together, played softball or flies and grounders when the weather was good enough, and every now and then saw a movie. But they did all of these things without Fergie. Sarah, who had known Fergie less than a year, was not as worried about him as Johnny was. "Maybe he's got a girlfriend or something," she told Johnny one day as they walked around the edge of Round Pond. "Or maybe he's just got other friends of his own."

Johnny shook his head. "He's got other friends, but none of them are really close to him. He plays ball with them and all, but they don't talk about the crazy kind of stuff that we used to." He picked up a pebble and skimmed it across the surface of Round Pond. It skipped four times, leaving expanding circles in its path.

"Anyhow, Mr. Ferguson's new job is turning out great," said Sarah. "He's selling used cars like nobody's business."

"I saw the story in the paper," Johnny said. A few days before, Mr. Ferguson's picture had been in the Duston Heights *Gazette* over a story that said he was the salesman of the month at Baxter Motors. "I even tried to call Fergie and ask him if he wanted an extra copy of the story."

"What happened?"

"He said 'No, thanks,' and hung up on me," said Johnny miserably.

Sarah stopped in her tracks. "Hung *up* on you?" she asked, her eyes blazing.

Johnny nodded. "I guess he didn't want to talk."

"Well, *I* guess he was just being a rude pest," returned Sarah tartly. "Dixon, friends like that you don't need."

Later, while he was home alone munching Ritz crackers spread with pimiento cream cheese, listening to music on the radio, and trying to read a book on ancient Mesopotamia, Johnny pondered Sarah's words. He thought back to the time when he and Fergie had first met, at a Boy Scout camp up at Lake Chocorua in the White Mountains. Fergie had been different from any friend that Johnny had ever had. Outgoing, happy-go-lucky, and devil-may-care, Fergie was willing to take any chance if he thought he would have a good time doing it. He and Johnny had gotten themselves into some pretty dangerous situations a time or two, but together they had always scraped through.

Up until now, anyway. Johnny sighed and closed his heavy book. Just then the music on the radio ended and a commercial began. An organ played a few bars of "Merrily We Roll Along," and then a fast-talking man said: "Friends, are you in the market for a great used car? We've got them by the dozen at Baxter Motors! Come and see our sweet deals, and then roll merrily along in your own set of wheels! Ask for me, George Ferguson, and get the best deal on wheels at Baxter Motors!" Johnny blinked. The voice was that of Fergie's father, but it sounded strange and different. Unlike his son, George Ferguson was a mild-mannered and soft-spoken fellow, but the high-pressure sales pitch made him sound insincere and conniving. Johnny sighed. Maybe Fergie and his whole family were changing somehow.

That evening after dinner he crossed Fillmore Street to visit Professor Childermass. The two of them broke out the trusty chess set, but neither played very well. After a few minutes Professor Childermass sighed, "My mind isn't on the game tonight. Call it a draw?"

"Okay," Johnny said.

They were sitting in the professor's living room, with the chessboard laid out on a card table between them. Professor Childermass drummed his fingers on the table and muttered, "I wish I hadn't already had my cigarette." He was trying to quit smoking, and had finally managed to cut back to only one of his foul-smelling Balkan Sobranies every day. He started to replace the chessmen in their wooden box, and then stopped, with a rook in each hand. "John, I suppose you deserve to hear the news, so I'll spill it. Dr. Coote has managed to dig up a little dirt on our friend Mr. Thanatos—not much, but what there is of it is wormy, slimy, and smelly."

Johnny swallowed. "What did he find?"

The professor finished packing away the chess pieces and stood up. "Let's go have some German chocolate cake first, and then I'll tell you." He led the way to the kitchen, where he and Johnny dug into two delicious slices of cake. Professor Childermass refused to say a word until his plate was clean. Then he pushed away from the table and said, "To begin with, old Thanatos had a much longer career than I'd imagined. Charley found references to his traveling medicine wagon as early as the 1840's, when he was operating primarily in western Connecticut and upstate New York. He was a snake-oil huckster, if you know what that means."

"I think I do," said Johnny. "That's a man who sells phony medicines, isn't it?"

"Bull's-eye, my friend. Thanatos peddled lotions and tonics, pulled teeth, and did a lot of unlicensed doctoring. He went from town to town in a gaudy wagon painted like a circus car and pulled by four white horses. He'd pitch his camp on the outskirts of some little town and spend a week or two there swindling every nincompoop in sight before pulling up stakes and rolling off to find his next victims. Funny thing, though—he never seemed to be in trouble with the law. Charley found reproductions of some of his posters in a crumbling old book about nineteenth-century advertising art, and that was all."

"Professor, how did he trick your father?" asked Johnny.

Professor Childermass scowled. "I heard the story a hundred times when I was a child. As I've told you, my father was an unusual man. He held not one, but three PhD degrees—in philosophy, history, and literature. I am told he is still a legend at Princeton University, where he taught literature for most of his career." The professor peered over the tops of his gold-rimmed spectacles at Johnny. "Please understand, I am telling you this so you will realize that Marcus Childermass was nobody's fool."

Johnny nodded. "I know he wasn't," he said. "He was a great teacher, and he was good with his hands too. I've seen the ship models he built from scratch."

The professor nodded and sighed. "Well, to make a long story short, my father was entering middle age around 1876. That's a time of life when many people begin to worry about growing old. It seems that he was at the family home in Vermont one summer when the celebrated Mr. Thanatos—or 'Doctor' Thanatos as the liar called himself—trundled into town. He gave a few men in town some most unusual presents. Mice."

"Mice?" Johnny asked. "L-like the one in—in that box that Dr. Coote showed us?"

Professor Childermass grunted. "Precisely like that one—but fresher. They *seemed* to be ordinary white mice. Thanatos claimed that he had stumbled upon an ancient recipe for the elixir of life—a marvelous magical mixture that would let a person stay young and healthy for hundreds of years. But there was a major hitch: The ingredients were terribly rare, extremely expensive, and frustratingly hard to come by. He had made just enough of the elixir, he told my father and the others, to test it on these mice. He gave one mouse apiece to half a dozen men in town and then vanished with his horses and wagon for ten long years."

"What happened?" asked Johnny.

"Absolutely nothing," said Professor Childermass. "The mice went on unchanged, day after day. One fellow in town, a banker, tried making his go without food and water. Six months later the mouse was still frisky, though it had become bad tempered. When he finally fed it again, it ate a whole pound of cheese in less than two weeks. Do you know what the life expectancy of a white mouse is, John?"

"No," said Johnny.

"About two or three years," replied the professor. "And yet here were these blasted rodents going along quite happily year after year. Well, the rest is obvious. In the early summer of 1886, when these creatures should have been dead, they were still alive and kicking. And that was when Doc Thanatos reappeared and reclaimed his infernal little pets. You can guess the rest. Everyone in town who knew about the miraculous mice was ready to put up hard-earned money to help Thanatos make enough of the elixir for them to have a swig.

My father invested five thousand dollars, quite a sum in those days. And within a few weeks, Thanatos utterly disappeared, leaving six very embarrassed middle-aged men in my hometown—and eight dozen more scattered all over New England." Professor Childermass shuddered. "And evidently one of his mice was never returned to him. That's the one we saw up at Charley's house."

"It must have been eighty years old," said Johnny.

"About that. Of course, I don't think the creature was actually alive anymore—not in a real sense. Thanatos found some kind of diabolical spell to make the mice *seem* normal, but they were no longer 'alive' as you and I would recognize living." The professor gestured. "They were like—oh, I don't know—like toys, almost, with movement and sound but no real spirit."

"Professor, you said that Thanatos tricked your father and those other men in 1886," said Johnny after a thoughtful pause. "Did you realize that was the very same year the McCorkle boy disappeared in Ellisboro?"

"Yes, and that's what made me think—"

The phone rang, interrupting the professor. With an irritated grimace, he went to answer it. A few minutes later he came back into the kitchen, a frown on his face. "I don't like this," he said. "I don't like it at all."

"What?" asked Johnny.

The professor poured himself another cup of coffee. "That was Charley Coote," he said. "He's been busy all day, poring over a dusty collection of old records. And he found something very unsettling."

Johnny felt a chill. "What was it?"

Slipping back into his chair, the professor took a long gulp of steaming coffee. "The passenger record of a sailing ship called the *Acheron*," he said. "It seems that it carried one Jarmyn Thanatos over from London. Except for one minor detail, that man seems to be our old friend."

"What detail?"

With a strained smile, Professor Childermass said, "Thanatos landed in Charleston in the year 1794. And he was described then in the passenger list as 'a gentleman about sixty years old.' "

Johnny blinked. "But that means—"

The professor's voice was dry: "Precisely. If that Thanatos was the same one as the rapscallion who swindled my father, then in 1886 he must have been about one hundred fifty years old."

CHAPTER SEVEN

That Friday, Professor Childermass and Johnny developed a plan. A plan that seemed to have little going for it, but the two were feeling somewhat desperate. The next day, the professor suggested, they would drive up to Ellisboro. "It's the one place where we suspect the rascal was operating for some time," the professor explained, "and it's just barely possible we may come across some trace of him. At this point, I'd say that anything would help."

"Can Sarah come along?" asked Johnny. "She's the one who found the newspaper stories."

"Hum," said the professor. "Yes-s, I agree with you. Sarah deserves to come along, so I'll call Dr. Channing and ask him. He's a pretty good fellow for an English teacher. I'll point out that it will be just a long day trip, and that Sarah really ought to learn more about our picturesque surroundings. But if her parents say no, then that ends the matter."

As it turned out, Dr. and Mrs. Channing said yes, and so very early the next morning, before the sun was even up, the professor stopped his maroon Pontiac in front of the Channings' modest home. Sarah came running out, wearing jeans, sneakers, and one of her colorful sweatshirts, this one white with crimson letters spelling out "Boston Red Sox" on it. The professor beamed. "You are adapting quite well to civilization, considering you came from the forsaken Midwest. Congratulations on your attire," he said cheerfully as she clambered into the front seat next to Johnny. "And let's hope our team doesn't leave us in the lurch this year, as they normally do. All set?" Everyone was, and they were off in a cloud of exhaust smoke.

The sun came up, shining behind them as they drove west on Route 2, and they stopped at a place called the Friendly Inn for breakfast shortly after turning north on Route 112. It was a homey little place, full of delightful smells of baking. They gobbled delicious stacks of pancakes drenched in butter and maple syrup, and then, full and happy, they traveled north into Vermont. As he drove, the professor talked about the history of the state, which he maintained was superior in every way to its neighbor to the east, New Hampshire. He gave a stirring account of the capture of Fort Ticonderoga in May 1775. The Revolutionary War hero Ethan Allen, together with Benedict Arnold (who was not yet a traitor) and eighty Green Mountain Boys had taken the fort from the British. The Americans held it for two years, and when a superior force of British soldiers had driven them out, a man named Seth Warner fought a brave rearguard action against the British that saved the Continental army, even though his small force went down in defeat.

As the professor went on and on about battles and armies, the Pontiac rolled through a green and increasingly hilly countryside. Soon they were skirting the beautiful Green Mountains. Now and again a sparkling blue lake appeared through the trees on either side of the highway, and the little white towns they passed gleamed in the morning light. The car's tires hummed along over the roadway as the sun climbed higher into a clear blue sky. Not long before noon they turned off the main highway and onto a winding, narrow road through the mountains. They came over a long rise, and before them they saw a lovely green valley. A small river twinkled in the sunlight, winding through the scattering of buildings and houses, and the road followed along the edge of the river. They passed farmhouses, then a small rural school, and then they clattered over an old arched stone bridge and were in Ellisboro itself.

They stopped in front of the town hall, a white clapboard building that looked almost like a church. Climbing out, the professor took a deep breath and stretched his arms luxuriously. "Smell that pure mountain air!" he said with enthusiasm.

Johnny took a sniff. It smelled like any other air to

him, though pleasantly cool and scented with the fresh aroma of growing things. Sarah just rolled her eyes.

They spent over an hour in the basement of the town hall, looking through musty old records. They found a few meager clues. Ellisboro, as it turned out, had sent quite a few of its young men to fight in the Union army during the Civil War. One was a certain "Jarmyn Nemo."

"Obviously a pseudonym," the professor announced. "Unless this is the father of that mysterious nephew who appeared in Duston Heights in 1886. I doubt that, though. It would be unlikely that brothers-in-law had the same unusual first name, and anyway it just sounds suspicious. You do know what 'nemo' means, don't you?"

"Sure," said Sarah. "It's the name of that submarine captain in the *20,000 Leagues Under the Sea* movie." The professor scowled at her, and she grinned mischievously and continued, "I read the book too. 'Nemo' also happens to mean 'nobody' in Latin."

"I am glad your father hasn't neglected your education," muttered the professor, a suspicion of a smile on his lips. "And you may not know it, but the Hebrew word 'adam' can just mean 'man.' So our fine-feathered friend Adam Nemo was literally the 'nobody man.' I suspect there was no such person as Jarmyn Nemo either."

"What does it say about him?" asked Sarah.

The professor adjusted his spectacles and peered at the yellowed pages of the old ledger. "Not very much. In 1862 he paid a substitute to fight in the Union army in his place. That was legal back then—though most patriotic people thought it was cowardly. That's about all."

They asked the city clerk about anyone named Thanatos, and the clerk, a big, bluff, hearty woman with curly white hair, blinked at the question. "Well, now, that's strange," she said in a deep voice. "I haven't thought about that old place in a dog's age, but yes, a man named Thanatos does own property in the valley. Although he hasn't lived here for thirty or forty years." She got out a huge book of maps and found one. "Here's the place," she said, putting her finger on the map. "It's just north of town. You go past the old mill and then turn left on the gravel road. It's about two miles down the road, on the right. Probably not much left of the place now, though. It's been empty for ages."

The professor had taken out a pocket notebook and was writing the directions down with his green Estabrook fountain pen. ". . . two miles, on the right," he muttered. "Thank you. You have been most helpful."

The woman raised her eyes and looked thoughtful. "You know, when I was a little girl, people believed that old place to be haunted. They called it the Spellbinder house and said an evil magician had built it back before the Civil War. It used to be a mark of courage for a boy to run up and touch the house and then run away. I don't s'pose kids do that kind of thing nowadays. Too much television, I say."

"How very odd. The Spellbinder house, eh? But Jarmyn Thanatos does own it?" asked the professor.

"That's what the records say." She pulled another heavy, green-bound ledger off a shelf and consulted it. "And he's paid the taxes on the place every year."

The professor craned his neck, trying to sneak a peek into the book. "Do you have a current address for this Mr. Thanatos?"

"Just a post-office box in Mount Tabor," she said, clapping the book shut in a puff of dust. "I'm sorry, but I really have other things to do. Good-bye, now."

That put the professor in a foul temper. He stomped out of the town hall muttering and complaining. It was time for lunch, and they ate ham and cheese sandwiches and potato chips at a small café between a pharmacy and a feed store. Then they piled into the Pontiac.

"Well, we can at least take a gander at the old Thanatos mansion," growled the professor, starting the car. "It's probably a fool's errand, but we've come this far already, so we might as well make our trip complete."

They drove slowly north, made the turn onto the gravel road, and rumbled along until Sarah spotted a roof back past the trees. A rutted, overgrown drive was just passable enough to let the professor pull the car off the road. They climbed out and he led the way forward, pushing through rank weeds and springy chest-high maple saplings. They suddenly came to the edge of a weird clearing, and they all stopped with a gasp.

A two-story wooden house stood before them. Once, it had been painted white, but the paint had flaked away except for a few leprous, scabby blotches on the weathered gray wood. Attached to the right side of the house was a tall tower, with arched openings in the top. They could see a great bell hanging there, a dark form against the blue sky of early afternoon. The windows of the house were broken and smeared with ancient dirt, and many of them had been boarded over. But the strangest thing about the place was that it stood in the center of a circle of death.

The earth was brown, dry, and littered with pebbles. Trees growing at the edge of the circle had lost every leaf and branch on the side toward the house. Grass came up to the invisible border and simply stopped. A perfect, bare circle maybe a hundred feet in diameter surrounded the house.

Johnny's jaw dropped. A bluebird had flown toward the house, but at the edge of the circle it chirped in alarm and swerved off to the left, as if aware that something unhealthy and uncanny waited ahead. On the bare earth, no ant crept, and in the hollow air, no birds sang.

"Well," began the professor, but his voice was shaky. He cleared his throat and started again, "Well, here we are. I don't know if our precious Doc Thanatos really was a wicked wizard or if he was just a cheating charlatan, but he certainly chose a home that was—ahem!— perfectly suited to him. It looks to me as if he put a lot of money into weed killer. I suppose I had better try the door, though it would astound the daylights out of me if anyone were at home in this dump. John and Sarah, you stay here and keep watch."

Johnny swallowed. Professor Childermass took a careful step forward into the blighted area, paused, and then strode to the front door, his footsteps crunching on the dry earth. He pounded the door with his fist, sending booming echoes throughout the clearing.

Nothing happened.

The professor went to one of the windows, shaded his eyes with his hands, and peered inside. Then he turned with a shrug and started back. "No one home—" he began.

"Oh, my gosh!" yelled Sarah. "Look at the bell!"

Johnny jerked his gaze upward. The black iron bell was moving, swinging slowly back and forth. Then it boomed out a terrible, loud peal. The sound stabbed into his ears, sharp and painful. The air itself seemed to vibrate with the overwhelming clamor. Johnny clapped his hands to his ears.

The professor froze in his tracks, wincing at the sound. He looked up toward the tower too and suddenly cried out.

A black cloud was swarming out of the arches. From it came a horrible droning hum, like the sound of thousands of huge flies. The living cloud whirled through the air, then dived at the professor. "Hornets! Run!" Johnny shrieked.

Professor Childermass needed no encouragement. He bolted toward them. The cloud of insects became a stream, diving straight for him. They enveloped him, swirling around him in a vicious whirlwind, and he stumbled, flailing his arms and yelping in distress. Sarah leaped forward to help, with Johnny at her heels.

Something hard slapped Johnny's cheek and exploded into dust, and then another and another and another. Johnny swatted, terrified that the hornets were going to sting him to death, but then he saw some of the insects clinging to his red windbreaker sleeve. They were not hornets at all, but some kind of locust, brown and brittle. "Ahh!" Johnny swatted them—and they exploded into ashy gray powder. They stank of mildew and decay. All Johnny's fear of dusty, crackly, dry things rose up in him, and he clenched his teeth to keep from shrieking in terror—to keep the horrible, scratchy, swarming things from scrambling right into his mouth.

They were *dead*! The millions of flying things were only shells, dry and hollow—and yet their wings buzzed and the creatures piled on, more and more, their dead legs scratching and scrabbling over his flesh, a maddening prickle over every inch of his exposed skin. Each one had almost no weight, but there were millions of them, more and more swarming onto him each second. He would be suffocated or—

Someone tugged his sleeve. In the center of a whirling murk of the little winged monsters, Johnny could hardly see, but he glimpsed Sarah's white sweatshirt, and he stumbled toward her. "Help me," she screamed. The professor had fallen to his knees and was trying to cover his head. He was completely black with the writhing, twitching forms of locusts. The terrible insect forms crept all over him, making him just a dark, writhing, shape.

Johnny forgot his own fear and brushed frantically at the awful things, gagging as they puffed into the sickening powder. "Come on!" he shouted. "We gotta get away from here!"

Wordlessly, the professor lurched to his feet, locusts falling from his arms. He wiped his face, threw a handful of the wriggling locusts to the ground, and staggered forward. Johnny pushed at his back, and Sarah pulled his hand in front. They reeled across the line where death began and life ended—

And with a whir that sounded like distant buzz saws, the cloud of horrible dead insects roiled away, flying back toward the house. Not a single one remained on them, although all three friends hysterically slapped at their arms and faces until they realized the nasty things had vanished, leaving behind only gray smears of greasy powder.

"Thank you," gasped the professor, leaning against a maple. He shivered. "I believe you two probably just saved my life. Ugh! That was like being attacked by an army of tiny little flying mummies! I can still feel them creeping over my skin." He took a deep breath. "I'm going to have about three boiling hot baths in disinfectant soap as soon as I get home. Those monstrosities have left me feeling defiled."

"L-look," said Sarah. "Oh, my gosh, look at the house!"

The professor made a strange, startled sound in his throat. Johnny stared, not believing his eyes. The desiccated locusts had swarmed all over the front wall of the house, but now they had arranged themselves into lines. The lines created ragged capital letters. And the letters spelled out an eerie warning:

THE FERGUSON
BOY IS MINE

CHAPTER EIGHT

If Johnny, Sarah, and the professor had seen Fergie late that night, they would have been shocked at his appearance. Over the preceding month, Fergie had become very thin and pale, and his eyes had a shifty, haunted look. At half past eleven that night, he slipped out of his house—something he had been doing several times a week for the last three or four weeks. He glanced at his father's pride and joy, a brand-new battleship-gray Studebaker that had taken the place of the old Ford. Fergie swallowed hard. His dad did not really like his new job. Mr. Baxter was a fast talker and a wheeler-dealer who didn't care if he cheated his customers now and again. But Mr. Ferguson was a great salesman, and he was earning good money for the first time in his life.

Miserably, Fergie hunched down into his black leather

jacket and trotted along the street. Only a few blocks away was a small park, between the river and the Baptist church that he and his parents sometimes attended. At night the park was always deserted. It was just a grassy rectangle, with a circle of thirteen ancient oak trees running around a central stone walk that in turn surrounded a fountain. Fergie went and stood beside the fountain, hearing the trickle of water. Stars winked in the dark sky overhead, and a waxing moon gave a ghostly light. Fergie felt himself cringing inside as he waited.

The tolling of the bells began. Church bells and clock bells throughout Duston Heights pealed midnight. But above them all, drowning out all the rest, Fergie heard the terrible deep booming of the bell only he could hear, the same bell that he heard anytime he used or even thought about the book.

In the darkness ahead, something glimmered. Fergie was breathing hard now, trying to control his panic. He knew what the white shape was—only too well.

"Good evening, my boy," said the voice with its faint British accent. It was the one Fergie had first heard in the library, back when he had sought out the book. The short, slight old man stepped forward. He was wearing a black overcoat, but his long fringe of white hair gleamed even in the dead of midnight. "Have you been practicing your lessons?" asked the man.

"Y-yeah," stammered Fergie. "Only it—it's not workin' out. Not the way you said it would."

"Oh?" In the darkness, the man smiled. Fergie could

barely make out his white teeth. "What trouble are you having, pray?"

Fergie squirmed. "Well—Dad has a new job an' he's doin' great at it, but he can't stand his boss. And Mom is worried 'cause Dad bought a new car an' a stove and refrigerator for the house, an' he's in debt. And they've been fighting about money." Fergie drew a long, miserable breath. "At least they never useta do that."

"Perhaps," said the man, "you merely haven't been specific enough in your wishes. Wishes are tricky, you know; you must manage them and show them who is boss. Now, if I were you, I could solve many of those problems rather neatly. I do not believe that your father's employer is married. If something were to happen to him, what would keep your father from taking over the business? And if he were in charge, then he would have no reason to dislike the boss, would he?"

Fergie closed his eyes. He could feel the pulse beating in his temples. "I couldn't wish for anything bad to happen to Mr. Baxter," he said.

"Oh? I could. But then, I hardly know the man. I never even heard of him before he hired your father, and I suppose you and Mr. Baxter are old friends."

"N-no," admitted Fergie.

"Well, there you are, then. You see, my boy, if I were in your position, I could very easily wish that Mr. Baxter would have some quick, painless, fatal accident. I daresay the world would not be much the worse for his passing."

"No," said Fergie. "I won't do it. That would be like murder."

"Very well," said the man. "But in time you may come to see my point of view. Now, time is fleeting. Let me teach you some special words. If you say them before you make a wish, you will find that you feel better and stronger. And they will help you to make some necessary wishes. Wishes that will put some former friends of yours in their place."

Fergie backed away. "I won't hurt my friends," he said.

"Oh, come," said the man in a soft, insinuating voice. "Can't you see that the snoopy old man is an enemy? Don't you know that the boy and girl you think are friends have already plotted against you? I think you should realize, my boy, that if you wish to become great, truly great, you will have to squash the insignificant insects that stand in your way."

"I don't want to squash anything," said Fergie helplessly.

The man laughed in a nasty way. "Don't you? Even if your so-called friends have been talking about you? Even if they have gone prying and spying into matters that are none of their business? Well, maybe you are not quite ready yet, but you are getting there—you are getting there. And you will have to move faster now than ever before. Since your conscience is so tender, I will not insist that you use your abilities—yet. Still, I think you should learn these words of power. Just tuck them away in your memory. You will know when it is time to use them." Then, patiently, the man began to repeat a string of Latin words to Fergie.

Fergie had studied some Latin in school, but he couldn't follow the meaning of the sentences the man made him memorize. For one thing, the words were not in the classical Latin of Cicero and Caesar, but in the vulgate Latin of medieval alchemists and sorcerers. But there was something else, something bizarre and disturbing, about the words. They seemed to have a weight and form of their own; dark, heavy shapes that lurched and slurched in Fergie's mind as he memorized them. He found his fists balling themselves in fury, he felt his face burning in hot anger, as one by one he committed the words to memory.

At last the man finished his recital. "I hope you have all that by heart. It won't be so good for you if you stumble over the words. Any questions?"

Dazed, as if he were waking from a trance, Fergie muttered, "Yeah—who are you, anyway?"

The old man took a step back, as if surprised. Then he chuckled. "Oh, you have seen my name in letters red as blood. And before too many changes of the moon, you will know who I am, all right. Yes, you will know with all your heart!"

The man waited, but Fergie stood biting his lip and not saying a word. "Good night, then," said the old man. "Tomorrow night, I think. Another lesson. There are too many enemies prying into my business, and I do not have the luxury of time. Go back home now, my boy, and sleep. Sleep and forget. But remember the name of

Adam Nemo. He will become very important in your life. He will become the only thing in your life. Go home and sleep." The man's voice was soft, hypnotic. Fergie swayed a little.

Then he blinked his eyes. He was alone in the park. Suddenly he was so weary, he could barely stumble off toward home. When he got there, he went to his room and dropped straight into bed without even taking off his clothes.

He lay in a strange state halfway between being awake and dreaming. When he closed his eyes, he saw blackness, but swirling in the blackness were fine red lines. These flowed together and became larger, until they were like writhing scarlet serpents. And then they became letters. Letters that formed two words, as red as blood on a velvet-black background:

Jarmyn Thanatos

Fergie sat up with a gasp. The old man who had met him at midnight to teach him strange spells was the same one who had written the ghastly *The Book of True Wishes*. But how could that be? Professor Childermass had claimed that the man had cheated his father seventy years ago. Thanatos would have to be well over a hundred if—

Settling back into bed, staring blindly into the darkness, Fergie wondered if it could be true. Was that why the weird old man seemed to hate and despise Professor

Childermass? Did he hold some ancient grudge against the whole family?

But what about Johnny and Sarah? Ever since the two boys had met, Johnny had always been Fergie's friend. Sarah was still pretty new in town—she had moved to Duston Heights from Iowa or someplace last summer, when her dad got a position on the Haggstrum College faculty. Still, Johnny, Sarah, and Fergie had enjoyed going places and doing things together, just as friends are supposed to. Feeling sorry for himself, Fergie had to admit that he didn't have too many friends—although he was athletic and self-assured, Fergie was just a little too smart-alecky and sarcastic to be a really popular kid. Fergie's mind wandered back to the good times and the bad that he had gone through with Johnny. He remembered times when they had been in tight places—even times when he had saved Johnny's life, or vice versa. But the old man had sneered at Johnny, and at the professor too. Fergie frowned. Could Thanatos have been right?

The more he thought about people talking behind his back, making fun of him and his family, the more angry Fergie got. Maybe it really was time to teach Johnny Dixon a lesson. Johnny thought he was so great, the son of the super military hero, Major Harrison Dixon. And Johnny was better at Latin and English than Fergie was too. Had Dixon been secretly laughing at him every time the two boys studied together? Did he privately think that Fergie was some kind of dimwit? Well, now Fergie knew a few things that Dixon didn't. Maybe it *would* be fun to put the wonderful Johnny Dixon in his place. Oh, nothing like the kinds of things that Thanatos had hinted. Nothing fatal. But maybe a little humiliation would teach Dixon—

The breath caught in Fergie's throat. He heard a soft sound, a dull, slow scraping sound, like a fingernail slowly rasping against wood. It might have been a mouse, or the wind brushing a branch against the house, but it wasn't. It came from the window. Fergie hesitated a moment. Then he tossed off his blankets and crept silently out of bed. He went to the window and raised it as silently as he could. The night was dark, but in the pale glow of the moon, he could see the quiet street. Nothing moved, not even a cat.

Fergie was about to close the window again, when something pale came trembling up over the sill and curled to grasp it. It was a hand. With a stifled yelp, Fergie jumped a yard backward. A second hand gripped the sill, and then a bloodless face rose, as if someone had climbed up the wall like a human fly and now was hauling himself in.

But the figure paused and stared at Fergie. Fergie's skin crawled. The face was the same one he had seen in his hideous dream about the bell tower—the face of the boy's ghost. The eyes were milky, even the irises, and the lips were so purple, they looked black in the dim light. "Don't listen!" moaned the apparition. "Don't believe him! He will steal your youth! He locked me away in the smothering dark! Lost, oh lost!"

Fergie felt goosebumps rising on his arms and on the

back of his neck. His teeth chattered. For a second he thought he was going to faint dead away, but then the figure simply faded, dissolving like a patch of mist in a breeze. It was gone.

Fergie switched on his light, moved a chair to the closet, and got the book down. He opened it and frantically tried to tear out the pages. Although the paper felt thin and fragile, it was tougher than any real paper could ever be. Fergie could not make even the smallest rip. He bit his lip, and then made a decision. He opened his bedroom door and listened. The house was silent.

Barefoot, Fergie tiptoed downstairs, into the kitchen, and then down into the cellar. The furnace was down here. Most places in Duston Heights had replaced the old coal-burning furnaces with oil-burning ones, but the Ferguson house still had an old coal burner. No fire burned there now, but a pile of dry kindling waited in a box on the floor. Fergie opened the iron door—it screeched on its hinges, making him flinch—and then tossed sticks of kindling into the furnace. He got a box of matches from a shelf and lit some small splinters in the pile. Soon the sticks caught fire, snapping and crackling as they began to blaze. As soon as the yellow flames were leaping up, Fergie carefully tossed the book right on the fire. He shut the fire door and hurried back upstairs.

Fergie closed his bedroom door behind him, locked it, and leaned on it. He felt like crying. He had given up great power. There were so many wishes left to make.

And yet he felt good too—he knew that somehow the book had been gaining control over him, making him its slave. Well, that was over at last.

With a sigh, Fergie clicked off the light and climbed into bed. But when he lay back, his head touched something flat and hard. He leaped out of bed, turned on the light again, and stared at his pillow. The book lay there, unscorched, safe and sound. And it was different. The black cloth looked darker, shinier, newer. The red letters of the title almost glowed with a baleful light of their own. Shuddering, Fergie stepped closer.

The book flopped open. Fergie blinked, and this time tears did come to his eyes. On the open pages was a stern warning. Fergie felt as if he were falling into a yawning, dark, bottomless pit. It was too late to save his friends now—too late to save himself.

The warning in the book was stark and plain:

If you try that again, you will die most horribly.

CHAPTER NINE

Right after church the next day, Johnny showed up at Fergie's house. Mrs. Ferguson smiled and said, "I don't think Byron's feeling very well today. He said he had a bad headache, so we let him sleep in. But maybe he's better now. You can go up and see if you want, Johnny. But watch out! He can be a bear in the mornings."

Worried as he was about his friend, Johnny couldn't help grinning. That was the old Fergie, all right—the worst waker-upper in the world. At Boy Scout camp it took everything short of a stick of dynamite to get him up in the early morning, and then he was grumpy and sore as a boil until he'd had a big breakfast. At least Johnny could be grateful that some things hadn't changed.

Johnny started up the stairs slowly, thinking about his

mission. He, Sarah, and the professor had returned to Duston Heights late the previous night. On the drive back, Professor Childermass had suggested that Johnny try to learn exactly how and where Fergie had come across the name Jarmyn Thanatos. "Something dire and pretty horrible is going on here," muttered the professor. "But until we know exactly what we're up against and how Thanatos has got at Byron, we haven't anything to fight."

"Professor," Johnny had asked in a small voice, "do you think maybe the man who's been paying the taxes on that place really is the same one who tricked your father?"

"Fiddlesticks," said the professor with a snort. "Also hogwash, applesauce, and horsefeathers! We know that an orphan boy called Adam Nemo changed his name to Jarmyn Thanatos a little more than sixty years ago. Obviously, that boy has grown up to be the modern Jarmyn Thanatos, now close to eighty years old. My grandfather used to tell me that you can't beat Annie Domini, John. Despite appearances, I still believe he was right."

"Annie Domini?" asked Sarah, sounding puzzled.

"My grandfather's little joke," replied the professor. "Anno Domini, better known as Father Time. No, John, what you have to do, and as soon as possible, is to see Byron and discover . . ."

And so here Johnny was, hesitating outside his friend's bedroom door. He raised his fist and gave a timid knock. From inside came a muffled voice: "Whazzit? Goway. Leamme lone."

"Hey, Fergie?" called Johnny. "It's me. Open up."

No answer. Johnny plodded downstairs. The smell of a roasted chicken met him, and Mrs. Ferguson stepped out into the hall from the kitchen. "Still asleep?" she asked. When Johnny nodded, she smiled. "Well, it's high time he got his bones out of bed. Stay for lunch, Johnny. I think Fergie's been by himself too much lately. You two haven't had a quarrel, have you?"

"No, Mrs. Ferguson," said Johnny truthfully. "It's just that Fergie's been kind of moody lately. I thought maybe something had happened at school or—" he broke off, too embarrassed to add the words "at home."

"I hope he isn't running with a bad crowd," said Mrs. Ferguson. She sighed. "You wash up. Lunch is almost ready, and I'll get Byron out of bed if I have to use a block and tackle."

Johnny washed his hands and went back downstairs, passing Mrs. Ferguson on the steps. She banged on Fergie's door until Fergie yelled, "Okay, okay, I'm up!" in a disgruntled voice.

"You've missed breakfast already. Now wash up, get dressed, and don't miss lunch!" snapped his mother.

At the foot of the stairs was a coat stand with a couple of raincoats hanging on it. Johnny slipped behind this and peered up the stairs. Mrs. Ferguson came down and vanished in the direction of the kitchen. Then Fergie's door opened and Fergie came stomping out. He was wearing green and white striped pajamas and carrying a pair of jeans and a white T-shirt wadded up under his arm. He yawned as he opened the bathroom door and went inside. A second later the shower began to run. Johnny tiptoed up the stairs and into Fergie's room.

He paused and looked around. Nothing had changed. Fergie's bed was a tangle of sheets and blankets, as if he had been wrestling with nightmares. His friend's desk was in its usual clutter of schoolbooks, library books, and miscellaneous junk. A baseball with a split cover rested next to Fergie's switchblade comb. The softball trophy that Fergie had won a few seasons back stood crowned with a golden plastic batter about to take a good hard swing. But the bat had broken off, and the softball player just looked a little stupid holding the stump. Next to the trophy was an Aurora model kit of the P-40 Flying Tiger airplane.

Johnny frowned. He remembered when Fergie had bought that kit, nearly six weeks earlier. Other finished models stood on clear plastic stands or dangled on strings from the ceiling: a B-17, a B-24, a German Stuka, a Japanese Zero, a P-47, and a blue U.S. Navy Corsair. Fergie was good at models, and he put them together within a day or two of buying them. But the P-40 was only half finished. The fuselage was wingless, and Fergie hadn't even started the paint job or applied the decals. A thin coating of dust covered the olive-drab plastic. Fergie hadn't touched the model for weeks.

But Johnny did not have time to worry about that. He felt like a sneak, but he had promised the professor to check for any evidence of Fergie's connection with the mysterious Mr. Thanatos. He quickly looked around, but he had no idea of what he was searching for.

Then he remembered Fergie's secret hiding place. Was it right to pry into something as private as that? Johnny decided he had no choice. He grabbed the chair and climbed up on it. He thrust his arm inside the closet and felt around. There was something in the cardboard compartment, all right. Johnny grabbed hold of it with his forefinger and thumb, fumbled it, and then got a better grip. He pulled out the book and stared down at it, feeling his flesh creep.

Part of the mystery was solved. There was the name he was looking for, right on the cover.

Suddenly, Johnny realized the sound of the shower had stopped some moments before. What if Fergie came in and caught him? He heard the bathroom door open.

With frantic haste, Johnny replaced the book, hopped down, and moved the chair over to the desk—just as Fergie opened his bedroom door. He froze with his hand on the knob, staring at Johnny.

"Hi," said Johnny, trying to make his voice light. He pretended to be leaning on the back of the chair. "So you're still putting the Flying Tiger together, huh?"

"Yeah." Fergie went to a drawer, took out a pair of socks, and tugged them on. Then he put on his sneakers. "Hey," he said suddenly, "is your dad still stationed at that base in Colorado?"

"Yeah," said Johnny. "But he may be coming home for a couple of weeks this—"

"You know what, John baby?" asked Fergie with a kind of rigid grin. "I think it would be great if you went out West to visit him. Ever thought about that?"

Johnny felt gooseflesh rising on his arms. Something was badly wrong. Fergie looked like himself, though thinner, with dark circles under his eyes, and he was trying to talk like himself, but the tone was false. "Uh," said Johnny, "I don't know if the Air Force would let me. He's in the Strategic Air Command, and his work's classified—"

"Go," urged Fergie. "Man, it would be so great, wouldn't it? You could see the Rockies, and maybe your dad would even take you skiing or something, and—"

"Come to lunch!" called Mrs. Ferguson from downstairs.

"Yeah, it'd be great," muttered Johnny, turning to go.

Fergie grabbed his arm above the elbow and held him back. "John baby, listen to me. I think you'd better go and visit your dad right now. This week. Or somethin' might happen—somethin' awful."

"Hey, let go," said Johnny. "You're hurting my arm."

"Come on—the jailer says soup's on," muttered Fergie bitterly. He pushed past Johnny and led the way downstairs.

Johnny hardly ate a bite. This meal was very different from the breakfast he had eaten with the Fergusons four or five weeks before. Mr. and Mrs. Ferguson hardly spoke to each other except to ask for the salt or the bread. Fergie stared at his plate and pushed his chicken and mashed potatoes around with his fork. Johnny felt like an intruder, not a guest. As soon as he decently could, he got up and said, "Well, I guess I'd better be getting home. Thank you for having me."

Mrs. Ferguson gave him a tight smile, but her eyes looked as if she were about to burst into tears.

Fergie walked outside with Johnny. "Think over what I suggested," he said. "I mean, your teachers would probably let you go an' all. It would be, like, an educational trip."

"Yeah," said Johnny. He got on his bike but didn't push off. He stood there, leaning on his left leg and staring at his friend. "Fergie, what's wrong with you? I mean, really. I know it sounds like kid stuff now, but up at Camp Chocorua we said we'd always be blood brothers and—"

Fergie's face turned red. "I don't have any brothers!" he snapped. "And neither do you!"

"Hey, take it easy—"

Fergie's eyes narrowed. "Say," he muttered in a low voice, "what th' heck were you doin' in my room, anyway?"

Johnny swallowed, but he knew his own face was getting red. It felt hot. "I was just waiting for you," he said. "Your mom said you—"

"You were spyin' on me!" snapped Fergie. He balled his fists. "Dixon, for two cents I'd teach you a lesson or three. Get out of here if you know what's good for you!"

"Fergie, calm down. I didn't—"

Fergie kicked the rear tire of Johnny's bike so hard that Johnny almost lost his balance and toppled over. "Johnny, get out of here!" he screamed. "I don't wanna do anything, but he's gonna make me!" His face twitched, and his expression became a mask of fury. "I hate spies! Go on, get out of here! You've got somethin' comin' to you, Dixon!" Fergie's voice suddenly changed. He sounded British as he yelled, "Get away, sir! I advise you to flee while you still are able!"

Johnny pushed away from the curb and pedaled for all he was worth. Before he turned, he glanced back. Fergie was standing in front of his house, arms stiff at his sides, fists clenched. But he seemed to have grown taller somehow, and his hair looked strange, as if it had grown long enough to curl over his shoulders. It might have been a trick of the light.

Johnny didn't think so. He rode his Schwinn in a frenzy of dread, heading for Fillmore Street, the professor, and safety.

CHAPTER TEN

"Blast it," grumbled Professor Childermass, peering out the front window for the fifteenth time. "Where *is* Charley, anyway?"

It was the first Wednesday evening in May, three days after Johnny's run-in with Fergie. Johnny had told the professor about how Fergie's voice had changed, how he sounded as if he were putting on a British accent. And as soon as Johnny blurted out the story of what he had found in Fergie's closet, the professor telephoned Dr. Coote. Dr. Coote had spoken to Johnny and had asked him to describe the strange book exactly, down to the last detail. And then he murmured, "Oh, dear. This is worse than I feared."

The professor and Dr. Coote conferred for a long time after that. Then Professor Childermass had sent

Johnny home. That was the beginning of days of worry. Monday hadn't been so bad, because that was the day of the May procession at St. Michael's School, and Johnny had been able to forget about his problems while singing in the choir and watching an eighth-grade girl crown the statue of the Blessed Virgin with a wreath of flowers. He had breathed the fragrant aroma of the Dei Gratia incense in the old church, had felt the joyful music calm him. Afterward, he paused to light a candle for his mother, and before leaving the church, Johnny had said a prayer for his friend Fergie.

Unfortunately his calm mood did not last. Tuesday was bad, with Johnny as jumpy as a cat. He could not keep his mind on his lessons, and Sister Theresa, his science teacher, had snapped at him most uncharacteristically. By Wednesday he was a nervous wreck. He told Sarah everything, and she commiserated with him. So after dinner that evening, Johnny had called her and she had come over to play chess with him. She wasn't terribly good at the game, but she was learning. Johnny won the first game and had been setting up the board for a second when Professor Childermass walked into the Dixons' dining room and asked the two young people to step over to his house. As they crossed the street, he explained that Dr. Coote had made some important discoveries and was on his way to Duston Heights right that minute.

That had been nearly an hour earlier. Johnny and Sarah had been sitting in the professor's living room ever since, and the professor was pacing the floor with growing impatience. Finally, at one minute past eight o'clock, a car creaked to a halt, and the professor rushed over to the window. "At last," he muttered. He hurried to the front door and a moment later ushered Dr. Coote in. Dr. Coote carried a briefcase and, though the night was warm, was wearing an overcoat and his battered old homburg hat. He took these off and hung them in the closet before sinking into an armchair with a grateful sigh.

"Spill it, Charley," growled the professor, hovering over him. "What have you found out?"

"Patience, Roderick," said Dr. Coote. "Heavens, but you're testy! Hello, Johnny and Sarah. I'm sorry the two of you are involved in this business. If I may say so, it looks, well, unpleasant. Most unpleasant indeed. And I am very much afraid that some unholy sorcery is at work."

"Charley!" snapped Professor Childermass. "Blast you, you always make us draw the story out of you inch by inch. Now, out with it! Exactly what have you found out about Jarmyn Thanatos and his blighted book?"

"All right, all right," grumbled Dr. Coote. He set the briefcase flat on his bony knees and opened it. He shuffled through a stack of photocopies inside and pulled out a folder, which he opened. It held a sheaf of handwritten notes on loose paper, and he began to leaf through these. "First of all, the name Thanatos is undoubtedly a false one."

Professor Childermass stared down at his friend. Then he stalked to a chair, collapsed into it, and very distinctly counted to ten. Then he exploded. "Of course it's a false one! We knew that already! You—you *pedant*, you!"

Dr. Coote adjusted his horn-rimmed spectacles on his long, bent nose and smiled. "Ah," he murmured. "But you don't know why it is false. You see, Thanatos was, or is, a practicing alchemist, and alchemists are known to adopt new names when they have experienced a personal transformation. However, I believe I have discovered the so-called Thanatos's *real* name. It is Jarmyn Cudbright. Does that name mean anything to you, Roderick?"

Professor Childermass glared. "No. Should it?"

"Well, you know of course about Theophrastus Bombastus von Hohenheim."

"Who?" asked the professor blankly.

Dr. Coote smiled broadly. "Why, Roderick, I thought surely you'd recognize *that* name. He was Swiss, and he was born about the year 1493 and died in 1541—"

Professor Childermass grew red in the face. "Confound it, Charley, why didn't you just use his other name? Everybody knows Philippus Aureolus Paracelsus!"

"Excuse me," said Sarah. "*I* don't."

The two men started at the sound of her voice, as if they had forgotten she and Johnny were there. Dr. Coote said, "Shall I tell her, Roderick?" When Professor Childermass nodded, Dr. Coote continued. "Well, Paracelsus was a physician and alchemist. He had a foul temper and was quarrelsome. Sometimes he even called his friends names." Dr. Coote peered at Professor Childermass. "Like some other people we know."

With great dignity, Professor Childermass said, "I don't have the faintest idea whom you mean, Dr. Coote!"

"Well, be that as it may," continued Dr. Coote, "Paracelsus really had some good ideas—he rejected the theory of humors, for example, which taught that disease was created by an imbalance in bodily fluids. Paracelsus thought, quite rightly, that disease was caused by outside forces, though he didn't come up with the notion of germs. Anyway, he was also an alchemist, and he hired a number of assistants, most of whom stayed with him for only a short time. One of them was a young Englishman named Jarmyn Cudbright, and he was different. Together, he and Paracelsus spent several fruitless years searching for the philosophers' stone. Do you know what that is?"

When Sarah did not answer, Johnny said, "It was kind of a magic stone that would change lead into gold, wasn't it?"

"Yes," said Dr. Coote slowly. "Except it was supposed to possess other virtues as well. It could confer great longevity, for example, and it could cure illnesses—at least, according to some authorities. Anyway, Paracelsus never discovered the philosophers' stone, nor did anyone else. But some time in the year 1535, Jarmyn Cudbright did steal a great number of his master's books and materials, and he vanished with them. About ten years later, he wrote a long, detailed letter to Michel de Nostre-dame, better known as the French prophet Nostrada-mus, in which he discussed secrets of foretelling the future. Cudbright turned up a few years after that in Great Britain, where he worked for some time with the magician Dr. John Dee. A few documents mention him during the early part of the seventeenth century. Then Cudbright disappears from the records until, um—" Dr. Coote shuffled through some papers—"until the 1720's, when he turns up again alive and well."

"Preposterous!" snapped Professor Childermass.

"Yet true. An astrologer and magician named Jarmyn Cudbright, who by that time was calling himself 'Dr. Thanatos,' was an associate of the notorious Count Alessandro di Cagliostro. You see what this means, of course."

"This Jarmyn Cudbright found some way of living forever," said Sarah slowly.

"Well—at least of living for a very long time," responded Dr. Coote. "Now, the odd thing is that the descriptions of Jarmyn Cudbright, or Thanatos, or whatever he calls himself, always disagree about his age. He looked younger in 1617 than he had twenty-five years earlier. By 1722 he was described as an aged man, and yet in 1758 he was 'a youth of twenty.' And when he boarded the *Acheron* to sail from London to Charleston in 1794, he was described as being 'about sixty.' Actually, he would have been about fifty-six, but some people—"

"Please, Charley," groaned the professor. "Get to the point, won't you?"

"Very well," said Dr. Coote, with an irritated glance at his friend. "On one occasion, right around the year 1778, Cudbright, or Thanatos or whatever you want to call him, was present at a meeting between Count Alessandro di Cagliostro and Comte de Saint-Germain. They were another two notorious alchemists and magicians, and the three of them discussed the elixir of life and a ritual by which a man could extend his life span to 5,557 years by periodically rejuvenating himself. My theory is that the ritual really worked. Now, only a garbled account of the process has been preserved—"

"A garbled account of garbage!" said Professor Childermass with a sneer. Then, before Dr. Coote could reply, he said, "Oh, Charley, don't jump to conclusions about magic and hocus-pocus. I think I know exactly what happened. There isn't just *one* Jarmyn Thanatos. There's a whole bunch of them, father and son, over the generations. Doesn't that seem reasonable to you?"

"No," said Dr. Coote. He handed a couple of sheets of paper to the professor. "Because I have here photographic reproductions of two letters he wrote, more than two hundred and fifty years apart. One letter is in French and the other in English, but as you can plainly see, the handwriting in both is exactly the same. Beyond any question, they were both written by the same man."

"Then how do you explain it?" asked Johnny, feeling a cold spot deep in his gut.

"I can only guess," replied Dr. Coote. "And my guess is pretty horrible. It's based on the case of Randolph Roberts, a Boston boy who seems to have been kidnapped in the early years of the nineteenth century. He was about fourteen or fifteen when he vanished. His parents were well-to-do, and they spent a year looking for him, running down every lead. At last they received a letter that told them their son was still alive and was in Charleston, South Carolina. They immediately left Boston to go there, but they met with an accident along the way and both were killed. Their will left everything to their son."

"Well?" asked Professor Childermass. "Was the boy alive?"

"*A* boy was alive," responded Dr. Coote. "He was found in a Charleston jail and brought back to Boston. He didn't look exactly like the Roberts boy—his head was shaved, and he was thinner. At any rate, people assumed his ordeal had changed his appearance. He told a wild tale about having been shanghaied by the crew of a sailing ship, then falling from a mast, hitting his head, and getting amnesia. Anyway, he had no relatives left, so he was put into an orphanage until 1811, when he turned twenty-one and inherited his parents' money. At that point, he moved away from Boston and vanished from the records. But there is another odd wrinkle to the story. In 1805, a few weeks after the young man returned to Boston, another Randolph Roberts showed up in Charleston, insisting that he was the legitimate heir to the estate. He said that a man whom he knew only as the Spellbinder had tricked him with a magic book and then had locked him in a sealed coffin to die, but he had managed to escape. Of course, no one believed him."

"Why not?" asked Sarah.

Solemnly, Dr. Coote said, "Because *this* Randolph Roberts was a sick old man in his sixties, that's why. He was put into some kind of institution, and he died within the year."

Professor Childermass sprang up from his chair. "Good God, Charley! If you're suggesting what I think you're suggesting, this is horrible! Do you mean that Jarmyn Thanatos is some kind of a—a time vampire?"

"What?" asked Sarah, sounding completely flummoxed.

Professor Childermass waved his arms. "Well, isn't it obvious? This Thanatos character waits until he begins to grow old. Then he causes some poor young boy to fall under his spell. Somehow or other, when the time is right, he—I don't know how, exactly—he steals their youth away! *He* becomes young, while *they* grow old and doddering. And then he starts all over again!"

Dr. Coote nodded slowly. "Yes," he said. "That's what I feel is happening here. It seems to take some time to work—half a year or so, usually. After that, well, I *think* the boy dies of old age—and Jarmyn Thanatos lives out the span of life the boy normally would have had. I'll wager that if you checked, you'd find a whole string of kidnapped boys in Europe and America over the ages. Even more, I daresay each and every one of them was a loner, without close friends. So this time, Jarmyn Thanatos just might have slipped up, because Fergie does have friends who care about him and who are willing to fight for him. I only hope our discovery is not too late."

Johnny shivered. He thought of his friend Fergie growing supernaturally old, becoming stooped and bony, his hair turning white and falling out. "We have to do something!" he exclaimed.

"We do indeed," said Professor Childermass decisively. "I'll be painted orange and called a pumpkin before I'll let that wretched wizard get away with this! But how the blazes do we fight him?"

"There is only one way," replied Dr. Coote. "The book that Johnny saw—*The Book of True Wishes*, I think he called it—is the key. That is undoubtedly a grimoire, a collection of terrible magic spells. Very likely as each one is completed, it increases the magician's hold over Fergie. In order to free our friend, you will have to destroy that book before it has completed its fiendish work."

"I'll rip it to shreds!" declared the professor. "I'll turn it to mush! I'll strip it to its covers and then use it to start a bonfire!"

Dr. Coote shook his head. "You will do no such thing, Roderick. In the first place, it's bound to have protective spells on it. I doubt if you even *could* harm it physically. Very likely something disagreeable would happen to you first, like the attack by those locusts you told me about. The only person who can really destroy the book is Fergie himself—or Thanatos, and of course *he* wouldn't do it. But there is a catch."

"What's that?" asked Johnny.

Spreading his hands, Dr. Coote said, "Well, usually these things can be destroyed in only one way. Fergie might not be able, say, to burn it at all. The key is to discover exactly what can be done to render the book harmless. And then the next hurdle is to persuade Fergie to do that—unless the book has him so thoroughly trapped by now that he won't even make the effort."

"But we have to try," said Professor Childermass.

Dr. Coote coughed. "Of course you do," he said softly. "Otherwise, Fergie and his family will die."

"His family?" Johnny heard his voice squeak in alarm.

Turning toward him, Dr. Coote nodded sadly. "Yes, of course. That is the pattern, you see. A boy vanishes, his family seeks him, and then the family dies too, leaving no trace. So I'm afraid that unless you act very quickly, all the Fergusons are doomed."

Just then the old Waterbury clock back in the kitchen bonged the half hour. The chime wasn't really loud, but everyone jumped, then looked at each other, eyes wide with fear. The clock had sounded too much like that other bell, the one in the belfry of the Spellbinder house. They all knew they were up against a force that was powerful, dark, and entirely evil.

CHAPTER ELEVEN

At a few minutes before midnight on Friday, Fergie once again slipped out of his house. He felt light-headed and dizzy. His legs were unsteady, as if the earth itself were rolling and pitching like the deck of a storm-tossed ship. The night was clear, and overhead a full moon hung, making everything look silvery and strange. Black, mysterious shadows pooled beneath trees. White houses glimmered like the ghosts of themselves. It was a warm night, but Fergie could not stop shivering.

Fergie clutched the book under his jacket, hugged against his chest. He took one slow step after another, passing the dim shape of the redbrick Baptist church, then hesitating at the edge of the ring of oaks. The gloom beneath them waited like a passageway into another world. A world of deadly mystery and magic. Finally, Fergie plunged into the shadows. He hesitated for a fraction of a second before stepping inside the moonlit circle at the park's center.

"So you have come at last." The old man waited there already, but now his voice no longer sounded kind. Slight and short, he stood with the moonlight lying on his long white hair and his shoulders like a silver cloak. But despite his size, he had the air of a cruel and powerful commander. He rasped out the words harshly, in a sneering tone. "The moon is in the proper phase for a great work of magic, boy. All you have to do is open the book, read, and make your wish—and your enemies will be dust beneath your feet. And you will have advanced one more step on the road to unimaginable power."

Fergie dragged the book out from under his jacket. He held it in his hands, and as the moonlight fell upon the cover the red letters of the title and the author's name began to glow with their own sinister crimson light. The book weighed a ton, and its covers were so cold that they numbed Fergie's fingers. He stood trembling, gasping for breath.

"Open the book!" The man's voice cracked like a whip. "Open it, I say!"

With fingers that felt dead, Fergie fumbled the book open. He had learned by now not to turn the pages one by one. They held some magic that prevented you from ever reading the same page twice. No matter how many leaves you turned, you never got to the beginning of the book—or to the end. There was always one more incredibly thin, incredibly tough page to turn. It was better to let the book have its own way, simply to allow it to fall open. Moonlight illuminated the pages now, making the black letters writhe in his vision. Fergie could read the words if he wanted to—but he desperately strove not to read them. For reading them meant death for Professor Childermass, Johnny, and Sarah.

"Read!" ordered Fergie's teacher. "I command it!"

Fergie shook his head and tried to yank his gaze away from the fatal words. "No," he groaned.

"Foolish boy! You know you want to show your power. You know the others have betrayed you. It is simple to extinguish them all at once—poof!—like three snuffed candles. They will be found lifeless tomorrow morning. The doctors will say the old man died of a heart attack, the boy and girl of some puzzling illness. It will be a great mystery. And only you will know the truth—that you used your mighty magic to wipe them off the face of the earth!"

"B-but it never works," croaked Fergie, his voice only a harsh rasp. He swallowed. "Dad hates his job. An' what about the last wish? I wished Mom didn't have to work so hard, an' then she fell on the stairs an' sprained her ankle. Now the doctor says she shouldn't get out of bed for at least three or four days—"

"Boy, you are trying my patience!" snapped the man. Then, with an ingratiating smile, he said, "Don't be weak, my lad. Once they called me the Spellbinder— because with words alone I could bind my enemies and deliver them to destruction. You could do the same, my fine young friend. Begin now, if you would be great.

Forget your family. They have never understood you or cared about you. And your so-called friends are spies and enemies. They deserve punishment, and only you can punish them. Read. Read now."

"No," insisted Fergie in a stubborn whisper. His throat felt as if it were being clogged with cotton. He shook his head.

Anger flashed in the Spellbinder's eyes. "Read, I tell you!" He pointed an imperious finger at the book. "I command you—read now!"

Fergie's face twitched. His arms jerked. His teeth chattered. He took long, sobbing gasps of breath. He felt as if the book were tugging at him, trying to pull him inside its bewitched pages, fighting him. His gaze unwillingly dropped to the first word of the first paragraph. "Th-th-the," he read slowly, his voice an agony of resistance. Then, with an effort greater than any he had ever made on the baseball diamond or the football field, he clapped the book shut. It made a dreadful sound—a sound exactly like the tolling of a bell. With a choking groan, Fergie dropped to the grass and lay there only half conscious. He stared upward into the dark sky, aware only of the white unblinking eye of the moon staring down at him.

Something came between him and the bright, cold disk. He felt warm breath on his face, breath that had a foul, sour stench. "So," growled the old man. "Still trying to be your own master, are you? You must learn, my fine young fellow. There can be only one master in the end—and he is the Spellbinder!" Fergie felt himself being lifted from the ground. Although the Spellbinder was old, he seemed remarkably strong. He carried Fergie as if he were carrying a stuffed doll. A doll with limp, useless arms and legs.

"Wh-wh-where—?" mumbled Fergie. The effort of speech was too great.

The Spellbinder gave a deep, hateful laugh. He was striding easily through the night, not even breathing hard from the exertion of carrying Fergie. "Where are you bound? To my secret hideaway, my fine young fellow! It's too early to begin the great spell, really, but you force me to do it. If I had known how stubborn you would prove, how strong your cursed will would be, I would have chosen the other one, the pale, frightened one. But no matter. You will learn all you will need to know later—knowledge that will last you for the rest of your very short life. Sleep now! I command it!"

Fergie's eyelids fluttered. It seemed to him that the moon shrank down to a tiny white point, flickered, and then went out. And then he was alone in darkness.

"So far, Dr. Coote hasn't found any way of destroying the blasted book. So I thought I'd better consult you," said Professor Childermass. He was sitting in the dark and rather gloomy parlor of St. Michael's rectory, talking to his old friend Father Thomas Higgins.

A tall, craggy-faced priest whose habitual expression was a scowl, Father Higgins listened sympathetically. "I wish I could help you, Roderick," he said. "But Fergie's mother is a hard-shell Baptist, and you know what they think of priests. According to Mrs. Ferguson, we're all secret agents of the pope, trying to waylay innocent young Protestants and force them to say the rosary!"

Professor Childermass sat on the sofa, leaning forward, with his hands clasped in front of him. "Oh, I'm not suggesting you go charging in with your chasuble billowing in the wind, swinging your thurible and brandishing a breviary," he said. "But there must be something you can do to help."

Father Higgins tapped his finger on his chin. "Well, an exorcism is out of the question, of course. You have to have the, ah, patient's consent, or that of the family. But I just might have heard or read something about dealing with books of evil magic. Let me see—it was a long time ago, when I was visiting an old cathedral in Ireland. The priest there showed me some ancient Celtic writing and said it had to do with using the four elements to destroy wicked writings." He was silent for a long time, and then at last he shrugged. "Sorry, Roderick, it's completely gone."

With a sigh, Professor Childermass rose from the sofa. "Well, Higgy, if you manage to recall anything more, please call me at once. I'm very uneasy about Byron, and I am getting more so with each passing minute. If you should—"

The doorbell rang. And then it rang again and again, frantically. The priest and the professor exchanged a startled look, and then both of them hurried to the door. Father Higgins threw it wide open. Johnny Dixon stood outside, his face a mask of despair. "Professor!"

he yelled. "Father Higgins! Something awful has happened!"

"Come in," said Father Higgins. Johnny blundered inside, and in the parlor he collapsed onto the sofa. He buried his face in his hands.

"For heaven's sake, John Michael," said the professor, "what's wrong?"

Johnny gulped and then sobbed, "We're too late. Fergie's gone!"

Father Higgins crossed over and put a kindly hand on Johnny's shoulder. "Calm down," he said in a reassuring, gentle tone. "Take a deep breath. Now tell us exactly what has happened to Fergie."

Johnny shook his head miserably. "That's just it—I don't know! Professor Childermass asked me to keep an eye on him, and so I've been riding past his house every afternoon after school's out. Well, this morning I was riding past, and Mrs. Ferguson came out, crying. She's hurt her ankle, and she could hardly walk, but she called me over and asked me where Fergie was. I told her I hadn't seen him, and she said he was missing. He hadn't even slept in his bed. Mr. Ferguson's called the police." Johnny gasped, and then turned to the professor. "Don't you see what this means? It's all just like Dr. Coote said—Dr. Thanatos has kidnapped Fergie. It's happening to him just like it happened to that Roberts boy and Tommy McCorkle."

"Oh, no, it isn't!" thundered Professor Childermass. "By heaven, that murderous miscreant has gone too far this time. John, I swear to you that I'll do everything in my power to save Byron. Even if it means going back to that lair of evil."

"B-but you c-can't—"

"Oh, yes I can!" roared the professor. "Let him send his winged mummies after me—I'll deal with them somehow! And I'll deal with our precious Dr. Thanatos too!"

"Th-then I'm going with you," said Johnny.

Professor Childermass frowned. "Now, wait a minute—"

"Johnny's right, Rod," said Father Higgins. He patted Johnny's shoulder. "Friendship wouldn't amount to very much if it didn't demand sacrifices and risks now and again. Count him in—and me too. I'll call old Father Manion to take my place at Mass. He's retired, but he likes to keep his hand in. Give me half an hour to arrange things and pack, and I'm with you."

So it was agreed. Johnny hurried home and told Gramma and Grampa that Fergie had run away from home and that he and the professor were going to see if they could track him down. Gramma looked worried. "Well," she said slowly, folding her hands over her flowered apron, "I guess y' can go, Johnny. But you be careful."

"It'll be all right, Kate," said Johnny's grampa, a tall, stooped old man with just a few strands of hair on his freckled, bald head. "Professor Childermass won't let anything bad happen to him. An' I don't think it'd be right to say no to Johnny, not when his best friend in th' whole world is missing."

Johnny telephoned Sarah, who wanted to travel to Vermont too, but he convinced her that her job was to stay in Duston Heights and keep track of events there. He arranged to call her that evening, and then he hurriedly threw some clothes into his old satchel. When Father Higgins arrived, Johnny climbed into the priest's big black Oldsmobile. Professor Childermass was already sitting in the front passenger seat, muttering complaints about their not taking his old reliable Pontiac. However, Father Higgins knew the professor's driving all too well, and he insisted on taking his own car.

"Well," he said when Johnny had settled in the backseat, "we're off." He put the car in gear, and as it began to roll forward the priest added in a worried undertone, "And may God and Saint Joseph help us!"

CHAPTER TWELVE

Even on a bright Saturday afternoon, the old house in the clearing looked threatening and sinister. "They came from up there," said Professor Childermass, pointing to the arched openings of the belfry. "Clouds and clouds of them—disgusting creatures! I don't think they can bite or sting, because none of them actually harmed us, but they're so numerous that they can crush us by sheer weight, or suffocate us by burying us with their own bodies."

"I see," said Father Higgins. He gave a sickly grin. "Well, I've been under fire before, but never from an army of insects! Let's see what we can do. I'm going to try to bless this place. And in my prayer, I'm going to put in a special word or two against Beelzebub. In the Bible, he's the Lord of Flies, you know. Maybe he's the

Lord of Dead Insects as well, and if so, I'm going to try to stuff every one of them down his evil throat. Wish me luck!"

Father Higgins opened a small satchel and took from it a purple stole, which he kissed and put around his neck. He grasped his breviary, the book containing the hymns, offices, and prayers for all the canonical hours, and in the other hand he held a rosary with a silver crucifix, which he looped around his neck and wore with the silver crucifix dangling like a pendant. He crossed himself, and so did Professor Childermass and Johnny. "You two stay here," said the priest. "If I get in trouble, come a-running!"

Praying in Latin, Father Higgins marched straight out across the dead, dry circle of earth. He stopped before the house and made the sign of blessing. The professor and Johnny heard his voice rise and fall, but they were watching the belfry for any sign of the marauding insect guardians. Both of them jumped when the black bell slowly moved and then sent its melancholy *bo-o-o-n-ng!* rolling through the clearing. "Oh, no!" groaned Johnny. "They're coming!"

"Thomas!" yelled Professor Childermass.

A humming, droning mass of flying brown creatures poured out of the belfry. The priest's voice rose in a stern rebuke, and Johnny caught the word "Beelzebub" repeated twice. The insects did not attack. Instead they rose to just above the height of the belfry and circled, more and more of them, until above the house buzzed a whirling disk of them. The cloud was so thick that it blotted out the sun, throwing the house into deep shadow. The incredible hordes of insects rushing from the belfry thinned to a stream, then to a trickle, and at last stopped. But millions of the creatures were in the air now, their wings setting up such a roar that it was almost painful.

Still Father Higgins continued his prayers. His voice swelled over the threatening hum of the insects. At last, the priest held his crucifix high and thundered a conclusion. And then, all at once, everything was still.

But only for a moment. Hundreds, thousands, millions of dead insect shells began to drift down. They pattered on the roof and on the bare earth like some infernal snowstorm. Father Higgins bowed his head and covered his face. The crackly, crunchy forms bounced off his hair and shoulders and fell to the ground. Within a few seconds, the clearing was more than ankle deep in them. And then they began to dissolve into powder. A gentle wind sprang up, and billows of dust smoked off the brown carpet, rising waist high. The wind scattered it into the woods on the far side of the house. By the time Father Higgins looked up again, almost no sign remained of the insect hordes.

The bell in the tower made a discordant noise, not a clear peal, but a flat *clunk!* Looking up at the belfry, Johnny yelped in surprise as an enormous triangular chunk of iron broke apart from the bell. It hit the edge of the arch and went spinning off to the right, where it struck the ground with a metallic clatter. The ruined bell looked as if some giant had taken a great bite out of it. Clearly it would never ring again.

"Come on," said Professor Childermass. Johnny followed him right up to the front door of the house. The professor clapped Father Higgins on the shoulder. "Way to pitch, Higgy!" he shouted, sounding as if he were cheering on the Red Sox. "You put the high, hard one right across the plate, and Beelzy went down swinging!"

"Thank God," said Father Higgins. "And now, since I suppose we must, let's check out this den of wickedness." He tried the doorknob. It screeched as he turned it, and the door groaned open on rusty hinges. Father Higgins replaced his priestly implements in his satchel, and Professor Childermass produced three chrome flashlights. Each of the three grasped one as they stepped inside the Spellbinder house.

For an hour they searched without finding anything more sinister than layers of dust, ancient swagging cobwebs, and empty, echoing rooms. The plaster ceilings had moldered, cracked, and fallen away from the laths in crunchy chunks. Mildew and water stains dimmed the tattered wallpaper and warped the wainscoting. The floors had buckled, and at every step grit crunched under their feet.

They put off the cellar until the end. Johnny really did not want to go down those rickety, half-rotten steps, but he took a deep breath and followed Father Higgins, with Professor Childermass coming behind as a rear guard. They found themselves in an earthy-smelling cavern of a cellar, completely empty except for a few rotten wooden boxes and barrels. Two barred windows, high in one wall, let a little murky daylight seep in. The walls were made of brick, and here and there green, slimy algae grew in streaks where water had leaked in. Father Higgins shone his flashlight all around. "Nothing to be discovered," he said. "Roderick, I'd say that your villain hasn't lived here in half a century or more. And he took everything with him when he went."

Professor Childermass had searched behind the furnace and had flashed his light over the coal bin, which held only a thin layer of black rubble. "It looks that way," he said. "But in that case, why did he leave those blasted magical bugs? You don't set a watchdog to guard a vacant lot."

Johnny was shining his light over the scummy walls, cringing because he had a horror of spiders. This cellar looked as if it would be a resort hotel for black widows and all their venomous kin. He noticed something unusual. "Is the wall caving in?" he asked.

Father Higgins went over to check it out. "A tree root has pushed through," he said. A whole vertical row of bricks had been shoved aside and now bulged out. The priest took hold of one and pulled at it. Then he leaped back as a brick avalanche began, a cascade of toppling bricks that sent up a dusty red cloud. He coughed and flashed his light at the rubble. "Maybe we'd better get out before this whole place comes down," he said. "I think—uh, oh. Better take a look at this."

With his heart pounding, Johnny came up beside the

priest, as Professor Childermass joined them. The collapsing bricks had revealed a cavity in the wall. It was a space perhaps four feet deep, three feet high, and eight feet long. And inside the opening lay a lead-colored metallic box.

"A coffin," said Professor Childermass in a low voice. "Well, now we know why the sinister sorcerer had those locusts on guard. He had a skeleton in his closet—or in his cellar. Let's get a better look."

The tree root was dry and dead, but in its years of growing, it had shoved the coffin lid partly aside. Professor Childermass climbed over the low mound of rubble and tried to peek through the opening between the lid and the coffin, but the space was too narrow. "Help me, Higgy," said the professor, pulling at more bricks.

"Don't call me that," grunted Father Higgins. "You know I hate it." He joined his friend, and the two men tugged and pulled until the whole vault was open. The priest looked a little sick. "I suppose we've got to try to haul it out," he said.

The professor nodded grimly. They seized the handle of the coffin and pulled. The root had grown down inside the foot—or was it the head?—of the coffin, and the box pivoted on this, grinding over the vault floor as it swung slowly outward. It stuck, and after some consultation, Professor Childermass suggested that they try to pull the lid off. "It's heavy, but I don't think it's screwed down. We can't push it back into the vault—there's not enough space for that. But we can pull it out into the cellar." He looked around and saw Johnny.

"John," he said kindly, "why don't you go upstairs and wait? This is a ghastly business for someone your age."

Johnny clenched his teeth and shook his head. "I want to stay," he said. He took a deep breath. "I—I'll hold the flashlight for you."

The professor nodded. For five minutes, he and Father Higgins tugged at the coffin lid, moving it a few inches at a time. Finally they pulled it loose and let it fall. It toppled onto the mound of bricks and lay upside down. Father Higgins shone his light into the coffin. "Poor devil," he said.

Johnny would never forget the pathetic skeleton. It was a dingy ivory color, with only six or seven worn-down yellow teeth in its fleshless jaws. A few strands of dry white hair clung to the skull. It wore the shredded remains of a black suit, the buttons made of corroded copper. The arms were bent back, with the fingers clutched in the air like claws. The finger bones were gnarled. "It was an old man," said Professor Childermass.

"People aren't buried in this position," said Father Higgins in a low, furious voice.

Johnny took a deep, shuddery breath. "He was buried alive."

"Yes," said Professor Childermass.

Father Higgins had bowed his head and was reciting the burial Mass. Johnny bowed his head. Then he saw something hideous. He bit his lip. As soon as the priest finished his prayers, Johnny blurted, "Look at the inside of the coffin lid!"

They all did. It had once been lined with red velvet, but the part of the lid that had covered the head and chest was bare. The poor victim had frantically clawed the fabric. Johnny imagined himself locked up in the airless dark of the coffin, struggling for breath—

But even more appalling, the dying man had left a message. Somehow, perhaps with a cuff link or even a button, he had scratched shaky letters into the metal of the coffin lid. There were two rows of them, the scrawl becoming worse as the message went on. In the glare of his flashlight, Johnny read the terrible inscription:

I AM TMCCORKLE
USEN ATHR TODE STRY BK

Late that afternoon, Johnny made a long-distance call to Sarah. He told her of the frightful discovery and the mysterious message, which the professor had carefully copied down in his pocket notebook. "Then we came here to Mount Tabor," Johnny finished, "because that's where Dr. Thanatos's return address was. But nobody here has ever heard of him."

"Well," said Sarah, "I've been doing some investigating too, and I think I can help there. Do you have something to write with?"

"Just a minute," said Johnny. They had stopped at a diner south of the little town of Mount Tabor, and the professor and Father Higgins were sitting at an outside table near the phone booth, glumly eating sandwiches. Johnny asked the professor to lend him his pocket notebook and a pencil, and then he picked up the receiver again. "Hi, Sarah?"

"Okay," she said. "Write down this name: Thomas Jannatry." She spelled it for him.

Johnny copied the name. "Who's he?"

"Oh, nobody special," said Sarah casually. "Just the mysterious old guy who caught a train to a town called Mesopotamia in Maine last night at 2:00 A.M., that's all."

"I don't get it," complained Johnny.

"I went down to the station," explained Sarah. "I thought maybe Fergie had caught a train, but he hadn't. Mr. Ferguson had already been there, they said. But I found out that Mr. Maggiore was working in the station last night, so I called him. He was kind of cranky, because he sleeps in the daytime, but he told me that the only person who boarded a train after ten o'clock last night was this Jannatry character. He was a short, skinny old guy with long white hair. And get this—he was carrying a great big black trunk."

"And?"

Sarah sounded exasperated. "And he wanted to haul the trunk on with him, but Mr. Maggiore said it had to go in the luggage car, so the guy filled out a slip, and he thought a long time before putting his name on it. The name was so odd that Mr. Maggiore remembered it. Look at the name, Dixon. Look at the letters."

Johnny studied the name. "I still don't see what's so odd about it."

"Come on, Dixon," said Sarah. "Try making an anagram out of the name."

Johnny thought for a few seconds, mentally rearranging the letters in *Thomas Jannatry*. There was a *J*, an *A*, an *R*—"Oh, my gosh," he said. "It's *Jarmyn Thanatos* rearranged."

"I'll give you a *C*, because it took you about five times as long as it did me. But you're right. Now tell the professor that the character you're looking for has hotfooted it to some bizarre place called Mesopotamia, Maine, and get a move on. And, Dixon? When you find the creep, give him a good swift one for me."

Johnny hung up without even saying good-bye, and he rushed out of the telephone booth waving the notebook and babbling. It took about half a minute for him to explain himself, and then everyone jumped into Father Higgins's Oldsmobile. They roared away from the diner with a screech of tires. They were off in search of Jarmyn Thanatos—and hoping they would not arrive too late to save Fergie.

CHAPTER THIRTEEN

"Watch it, Rod!" shouted Father Higgins. It was late at night, and Professor Childermass had taken over the driving duties. The big Oldsmobile was barreling through New Hampshire, heading into Maine, but the professor drove this car no better than he drove his Pontiac. The Oldsmobile clattered, jerked, and skidded in tight turns, while Father Higgins held on and muttered prayers under his breath.

Professor Childermass did not reply. He leaned forward over the steering wheel, as if he could push the car a little harder that way. "We just passed through Berlin," he announced. "We'll be in Maine in a few minutes. Let me see—Gilead, then Bethel. Then north to Newry, and seventeen miles past Newry, Mesopotamia. That scoundrel certainly chose a forsaken countryside to hide in."

Johnny was trying to keep from being jounced off the backseat. "P-professor," he said, "th-that isn't t-too far from—"

"From Lake Umbagog and my late brother Perry's old estate," said Professor Childermass grimly. "I noticed the irony, John."

"I don't think I've heard much about your brother," said Father Higgins, with the tone of someone trying to take his mind off his present danger.

"There isn't a lot to tell," returned the professor. "Peregrine Pickle Childermass was a bit of a scatterbrain, a rich man, and a dabbler in things he should have left alone."

"Oh," said Father Higgins. "Totally unlike you."

"That's right," said the professor. "Actually, a few good things have come out of Maine, though I wouldn't number my late lamented brother among them. There was Louis Sockalexis, for instance. He was a Penobscot Indian who played baseball for the Cleveland Spiders before the turn of the century. A real slugger. Later, they gave the Cleveland Indians their name in honor of Sockalexis. He had a brother who was a wonderful runner—" The tires bawled as the professor almost lost control of the car in a curve.

"Rod!" shouted Father Higgins. "*Please* watch the road!"

"Oh, very well," muttered the professor, and he hunched over even farther. They drove into western Maine on Highway 2, and eventually they turned north. Even with a brilliant moon out, Johnny couldn't see much, but he knew that this was a mountainous part of Maine, where the roads twisted and turned, rose and fell, through peaks covered with evergreens, birch, and beech trees. He had dozed a little, but now he was wide awake. His luminous watch said it was past one in the morning.

The car jounced over a gravel road for what seemed like a long time but probably was half an hour or less. Then they were on pavement again, and at last the professor said, "Here we are, you two. The wonderful Mesopotamia, Maine, as dreary a little burg as you're likely to find. And naturally everything is closed."

Johnny looked out the car window. Mesopotamia was a little cluster of wood frame and brick buildings. He saw a hardware store, a drugstore, a general store, and a grocery, but as the professor had observed, they were all closed and silent. "I know one thing that will be open," said Johnny. "The train station."

"My thought exactly," answered the professor. He drove a little farther until he spotted the station, and then he parked the Oldsmobile in a gravel lot. They all climbed out, stretching their cramped arms and legs, and crunched over the gravel to the station, a modest clapboard affair painted a dull yellow. The moonlight gleamed in long, silver lines on the railroad tracks just the other side of the station.

They pushed through a door and found themselves in a small waiting room. Four benches, like church pews, stood around empty. A tall green candy machine and a red soft-drink machine stood against the far wall next to the big doors that opened onto the platform, and doors to the men's and women's rooms were on the left. To the right was a counter that opened through into another room. Behind the counter, a short, potbellied, balding man of about fifty was asleep in a wooden chair. He had the chair tilted back against a filing cabinet, and his feet were propped on a small black cast-iron stove. The man wore a green celluloid eyeshade that cast a green shadow over his long nose, scraggly black mustache, and weak chin.

"Service!" roared the professor, clapping his hand down flat on the counter.

The man jumped at the sound, scrambled up from his chair, and hurried to the counter. "Sorry, sorry," he said, rubbing his palm over his face. "Didn't see you come in. Yes, yes, what'll it be for you fellas?"

"Just a little information," said Father Higgins, pushing in front of Professor Childermass. "Early yesterday morning, a long-haired old man got off the train here. He had a great big trunk with him. Did you notice him?"

"Hum," said the stationmaster. "That woulda been old Mr. Omen. Yep, I recall he got off the mornin' train, all right. He hauled that trunk out to his car himself—wouldn't let me touch it."

"Where does the villain live?" asked the professor in a voice like the first rumble of an earthquake.

The stationmaster backed away. "Say, who are you men, anyways? And who's that boy?" He narrowed his brown eyes. "Seems t' me we had a bulletin t' look out for a runaway kid."

Professor Childermass swelled like a frog. "You are

wasting our time, your time, and perhaps the life of the very boy you read about! Sir, if I have to, I will come behind that counter and persuade you myself, but before we leave here, you will tell us where this so-called 'Omen' lives!"

The little man looked alarmed. His eyes grew round, and he tugged nervously at his shaggy black mustache. "Now, now, don't get all in a lather. Why, that old fellow's a character in these parts. Yessir, a real character. His name's Armyn J. Omen, an' he lives in the old huntin' and fishin' lodge, out toward Lake Mooselookmeguntic. You go north on th' gravel road, up the side o' Camelback Mountain and across Black Bear Notch. Then you follow the road, oh, I dunno, about three, four miles, an' you'll see a dirt road on your left that turns off to the west. Well, y' take that until you cross th' old bridge—you'll know it when you come t' it—an' then look sharp for a lane that cuts off to th' right. It goes straight to th' old Mooselookmeguntic Lodge."

"Thank you," said Father Higgins, and he hustled the professor out to the Oldsmobile before anything more could be said. "I'll drive," the priest announced. "Roderick, you should watch your temper. It's a wonder that fellow told us anything, the way you blew up at him. You can catch more flies with honey than with vinegar, you know."

"Phooey!" erupted the professor, yanking open the passenger's door. "Who wants a handful of sweet, sticky flies?"

Sighing, Father Higgins started the car. "I suppose," he said, "you noticed the clever alias."

"Yes, yes, of course," grumbled the professor. "*Armyn J. Omen* is an anagram of *Jarmyn Nemo*. Even though he doesn't possess much imagination, our precious Dr. Thanatos has more names than Heinz has pickles!"

"Now, there is a welcome sight," said Father Higgins. They had passed through most of the town, but ahead on the left was a little motel, a flat-roofed, U-shaped building with only about a dozen units. Its blue-and-red neon sign said it was the Mesopotamia Inn and that it had vacancies. Father Higgins drove into the motel parking lot.

"What in the world are you doing?" asked the professor.

"Roderick," the priest said patiently, "it is the middle of the night. Even if we can find this place, we can't see much, and if we use lights, we'll give ourselves away. I think our best plan is to snag a little sleep, start out again at daybreak, and get there in the early morning. At least then we'll have some faint hope of catching Thanatos by surprise. I very much doubt that he's hurt Fergie—yet. He had no idea that Sarah would be so quick to track down his movements. From what you found out, he must think anyone looking for him would head for his old stamping grounds in Vermont, not to his hideout in Maine. As far as Thanatos knows, he got away from Duston Heights scot-free, and no one there has an inkling of who he really is."

After some grumping, the professor gave in. They

rented a room with two regular beds and a Murphy bed, which is the kind of bed that folds up into a compartment in the wall. Although both men were world-champion snorers, Johnny was so sleepy that he conked out at once. Not even the fear of what they might find at the end of their journey could keep him awake—but he tossed now and then with bad dreams about the malicious Dr. Thanatos.

One dream in particular was odd. He thought he was playing Pickup Sticks with a sad-faced boy a little younger than he was. The game never really got started, though, because the other boy kept bunching up the sticks and tossing them onto the ground. "It's hard to make sense in the dark," the boy complained.

Johnny had no idea what he was talking about. But he noticed that every time the sticks clattered to the floor, they formed patterns. Something about the patterns almost had meaning. But the boy always picked the sticks up and threw them down before Johnny could make heads or tails of them. "Who are you?" Johnny asked.

"I'm nobody," answered the boy. "I was someone, but he made me nobody." He threw the sticks down again, and they clattered very loudly.

Johnny looked at them. They had become miniature bones, ribs and femurs and humeri. And they fell together to spell out the word *NEMO*. The boy reached to pick them up again.

With a gasp, Johnny saw that the bones had become thin sticks again—but the boy's hand was a skeleton's hand. He looked up, into the empty eye sockets of the aged skeleton he had seen in the coffin. The skeleton's jaw opened and closed, and the boy's voice came from the fleshless mouth: "He locked me in the dark. I tried to dig my way out, but I was too weak, too weak! Remember the four elements!" And then the skeleton flung the sticks one last time.

They landed in the pattern of the letters that had been scratched on the inside of the coffin lid. Everything grew dark, but the letters glowed with a faint light of their own. Johnny reached to pick up the sticks and his hand hit something smooth and hard, something made of metal. He flattened his hand against it and realized that the sticks had become scratches. And somehow now they were above him—

He was locked inside a coffin.

With all of his strength, Johnny pushed at the lid, but it was shut fast. He couldn't budge it. His chest heaved. The air was running out. And now the letters were writhing, coming to life, becoming those horrible dry husks of insects. They crept about just above him, and then dropped onto his face—

He screamed and sat up. The professor and Father Higgins were already up and dressed, and they stared at him. Milky morning light came through the motel room window. It was daybreak, and they were ready to attack Dr. Thanatos in his stronghold.

CHAPTER FOURTEEN

"May all the saints have mercy on us," said Father Higgins softly. The gravel road had become narrower and narrower as it twisted up the flank of Camelback Mountain. It crested at Black Bear Notch, and then started down again—but Black Bear Notch was barely wide enough for the Oldsmobile to creep over. Johnny cringed. To his left, the mountainside fell away in a sheer five-hundred-foot drop. The cliff side was weathered gray granite, streaked with black patches of darker stone and blotchy with the pale green rings of lichens. From a cleft in the stones far below, a waterfall leaped out to tumble down in a series of cascades, ending in a snaky black stream that wound through a dense forest. A few rocks crumbled away as Father Higgins eased the car through the pass.

Then they all took a deep breath. The road twisted down again, and they gathered speed. "Three miles," announced Professor Childermass, who was watching the odometer with the eye of a hawk. "Watch for that dirt road, Thomas."

"I'm watching, Roderick," said Father Higgins. But the stationmaster's directions were a little off. The Oldsmobile rolled through a desolate countryside, where ruined foundations and isolated, broken chimneys marked old, deserted farms. Even a stretch of rhyming Burma Shave signs alongside the road looked weathered and abandoned. No car met or passed the Oldsmobile, and Johnny saw no trace of any living being. They drove almost another three miles before the dirt road cut away to the left. Father Higgins made the turn, and the car bounced and creaked along a rutted country lane, weeds brushing both sides. The lane still went downhill. They crawled at about twenty miles per hour for a good distance, and at last the road began to level. "There's the bridge up ahead," Father Higgins said. "Do you think it's safe, Roderick?"

"I think we'd better inspect it," replied the professor. The span looked ancient. It was a rickety, swaybacked wooden structure built on four piers of rounded brown river stones and was only about thirty feet long. The water underneath was very dark, almost black in the early light. Professor Childermass walked onto the bridge, stamped his feet, took a deep breath, and said, "It may hold us, or it may not. I suggest that you and John cross on foot, and I'll drive the car over."

"Get out, Johnny," said Father Higgins. "You go on. I'll drive the car myself. If it plunges into the drink, at least I'll be the one responsible for it, and not Rod." Johnny climbed out and joined the professor, who groused a little, but they both crossed over the bridge. The Oldsmobile moved forward foot by foot. The bridge was so narrow that the big car almost scraped the rails on either side. The old boards creaked and crackled and sagged, but they held up, and after what seemed like an agonizing time, the car was across.

"Now," said the professor as he and Johnny climbed back in, "I spy with my little eye something that looks like an old signboard up ahead. Let's see what it says." They drove slowly forward. The signpost leaned drunkenly from a thick tangle of blackberry vines, sun-faded to a dismal gray with just a few traces of white letters still visible:

MO   ELOOK   C LODG

A ghostly arrow pointed down a badly overgrown lane on the right.

"This is it," said the professor. "I can see where the weeds were crushed down recently. That must have been when our friend with the trunk drove this way. I suggest that we get the car off the road, then proceed on foot. It isn't even seven-thirty yet, and we may take the fiend by surprise."

They walked single file down the overgrown lane. Weeds, wet with dew, slapped against them. Cobwebs, invisible until they stuck to their faces, lay across their path. They turned a curve, and ahead of them they saw a big log cabin. It was two stories tall, with a row of six gables across the front, and it had a couple of stone chimneys. The roof had been covered with gray cedar shingles, but dozens of these had blown off, leaving irregular bare spots. Patches of green moss spattered the roof and the dark brown walls. A sagging porch ran across the front and above it was a sign, which read *Mooselookmeguntic Lodge*. A tall wooden tower stood near the cabin, and about a hundred yards behind, a dark, misty lake lapped at a derelict old pier that had half fallen into the water.

Father Higgins was leading the way. He crouched low, and Professor Childermass and Johnny stooped behind him. "Well, Roderick?" asked the priest. "You're the military expert. How do we attack?"

"I was in intelligence, not the infantry," returned the professor. "However, I think our best approach would be to follow the hillside on the left. The trees there will give us cover. We'll come out on the chimney side of the house, which looks like a blind spot. Let's go. Space yourselves out so that Father Higgins is about twenty feet ahead of you, John. I'll bring up the rear."

They carefully and quietly snuck through a ruined apple orchard, the trees all wild and long unpruned. Small green apples, most of them already worm-eaten, clung to the gnarled branches. Then they emerged very close to the house. "Ah-ha," whispered the professor. He pointed, and Johnny saw the long black hood of an old car projecting from behind the house.

"A Duesenberg," said Father Higgins. "A real antique—it must be thirty years old."

"But it has a big, powerful engine. Just right for hauling mysterious trunks. I'm going to take a look." The professor darted forward in a series of short runs. He reached the corner of the lodge, peered around, and stiffened. "Oh, my God!" he exclaimed. "Come quick!"

The other two ran to join him. Johnny saw what had startled the professor, and he felt his heart sink. A low mound of dirt, six feet long and three feet wide, was just behind the lodge. A pick and shovel were stuck into the freshly turned earth. The same thought flashed through all three minds at once. Without a word, the professor and Father Higgins seized the tools and began to dig with frenzied haste. The clammy, wormy scent of moist soil filled Johnny's nose. *Chunk! Thud!* The pick and shovel bit deeper and deeper into the earth. Then the spade shrieked against something metal. It was not very deep, only a couple of feet down. The professor used the shovel to clear all the dirt off the top of a metal coffin. "Help me!" he shouted. Father Higgins stooped and put the point of the pick under the edge of the coffin lid. Then he pulled back with all his strength, using the pick like a lever. The lid sprang open.

Johnny screamed. His friend Fergie lay inside the coffin, his arms folded, a black book clutched to his chest. His eyes were closed, his face was pale, and his hair had turned completely white.

CHAPTER FIFTEEN

"He's breathing!" yelled the professor. He and Father Higgins lifted Fergie out of the coffin. They lay him on the grass. Fergie was wearing his motorcycle jacket, jeans, and boots. Except for his hair, he didn't look any different.

"The spell isn't complete," said Father Higgins. He patted Fergie's face. "Byron! Wake up!" No response. More loudly, the priest said, "Byron Ferguson! This is your baseball coach. We've got two men out in the ninth, and we're one run behind. Go to bat now!"

Fergie stirred slightly, but his eyes did not open. Something moved at the edge of Johnny's vision. He turned around, startled, and yelled in surprise, "Look! That must be him!"

A dark figure was climbing the ladder of the wooden

tower. It was a small, slight man, dressed in black. His long hair was iron-gray and curled down over his shoulders. He glared down at them as he climbed, his mouth set in a grimace of hatred. Professor Childermass stood up straight, brandishing the spade. "You!" he shouted. "Doctor Jarmyn Thanatos! Stop where you are!"

"Fools!" yelled the climbing figure. "You're too late to stop me! No one can stop me now! The process has begun! Begone, I say, or else you will wish you had never been born!" He reached a platform at the top of the tower and stretched up an arm.

"You're the one who'll be sorry!" returned the professor. "Give yourself up. If I have to burn down that tower to get you, I'll do it—Jarmyn Cudbright!"

The climbing man reeled, as if he had almost fallen. He threw back his head and howled, a long animal sound. Then his stretched-out hand found what he was searching for, and he tugged a rope. A bell clanged.

Johnny put his hands tight over his ears, but the sound made the ground shake as though an earthquake were rolling through. Professor Childermass staggered and fell, and Father Higgins collapsed to his knees. "I am the master of bells!" sang Thanatos in a triumphant voice. "I can make the clamor still you or kill you! And know, old fool, that fire is not the element that can stop me. Have a taste of darkness and death, you interfering insects!" He yanked the rope again, and the bell sounded. Johnny screamed, but he could not even hear his own voice over the terrible noise. The world turned dark. He was blacking out.

And when all was dark, a strange thing happened. He saw those glowing lines again, the letters the doomed Tommy McCorkle had scratched into the lid of the death-trap coffin. But this time they fell together and made sense. This time Johnny knew what he had to do.

USEW ATHR TODE STRY BK. A nonsense jumble of letters. But allowing for the darkness, allowing for the trapped Tommy McCorkle's terror, the letters would make sense if you looked at them a little differently. He must have been running out of air. He put some strokes in the wrong places because he couldn't see, and he abbreviated the last few words. The answer was in one of the ancient four elements. Not air. Not earth. Not fire. But—

USE WATER TO DESTROY BOOK.

Water! And only a hundred yards away was a whole lake of it!

The darkness parted like clouds rolling away. Professor Childermass lay on the grass, unconscious. A dazed Father Higgins was pushing himself up from the ground. It was up to Johnny.

He grabbed the book and tore it from Fergie's grasp. He clutched it like a football and ran for his life. Behind him he heard Thanatos screech in fury: "Get him! Stop him! I command you!"

Johnny had never been any good at football. He was winded even before he was halfway to the dock. Then he heard footsteps pounding close behind. Thanatos? He couldn't look around. He put on a new burst of speed. He ran out to the edge of the sagging dock—

Whump! Someone tackled him, sending him sprawling. His glasses flew off, and he lost his hold on the book. It skidded across a patch of sand and came to rest on the first plank of the half-ruined pier. Johnny rolled and squirmed, and he saw that the person who had grabbed him was—

"Fergie!"

"The book!" croaked Fergie in an awful old-man's voice. "I must save the book!" He pushed Johnny aside.

Johnny turned to scream for help, but what he saw froze him. Thanatos had spread his arms, holding his cloak out to the sides. Leaping from the tower, he seemed to glide like a bat. He soared through the air, over the unconscious Professor Childermass, over the reeling Father Higgins. He landed twenty feet away, his thin face writhing, his hands clenched like twisted, bony claws. "Boy, I will torment you worse than your worst nightmares!"

Johnny looked around fearfully. Fergie had retrieved the book. He stood there clutching it to his chest. His eyes were blank and mindless. No help there.

Or was there? With a sudden crazy inspiration, Johnny tore off his windbreaker and kicked off his shoes. He ran past Fergie. "Last one in's a rotten egg!" he shouted, and he did a passable cannonball. *Splash!* He came up gasping—the water was icy! Fergie had turned and stared down at him.

"Hey, chicken!" shouted Johnny. "C'mon in. It's *freezing*, man! Betcha won't come!"

Fergie took an uncertain step onto the swaying pier.

Behind him, Thanatos stopped, his arm stretched out. "Here!" he shrieked. "Here, I command you!"

Fergie stopped.

Desperately, Johnny shouted, "C'mon, you big fat chicken. I dare you. I *double* dare you! Let's see that famous Ferguson swan dive! Or are you chicken? Buck-buck-buck!"

Something snapped in Fergie. With an inarticulate cry, he took three running steps and went off the pier, headfirst. Thanatos leaped forward—

Fergie went into the water as smoothly as if he were in his swim trunks, not his motorcycle outfit. He came up like a porpoise, his eyes wide in shock and astonishment. In his hands, the book melted. It ran in a black, chunky rivulet through his fingers, looking like dirty, clotted motor oil.

And on the shore, the running figure of Thanatos melted too. His features flowed and ran. An ear slipped down the side of his neck. His nose dripped across his chin. The flesh on his outstretched arm drooled away, leaving a bare bone, and then that flowed like white wax. In two steps he was a dissolving lump, and in another second he was a greasy, gray puddle.

"Man!" said Fergie in a stunned voice. "What happened?"

Johnny looked at his friend and shouted in joy. Fergie's hair was growing darker. It was pale gray, then iron-gray, and finally black and curly. The two boys floundered up to the shore. Father Higgins was there already, holding Johnny's glasses in his left hand, reaching out his right to help them, and close behind him was the professor, still carrying the shovel. As soon as the shivering boys were out of the water, Professor Childermass stared in disgust at the messy puddle that had been Jarmyn Thanatos. He scooped up shovel after shovel of it and flung it into the lake. When the earth was clean again, he said, "Johnny, you've got extra clothes in the car. What we're going to do about you, Byron, I don't know, but we'll find some way to keep you from freezing to death. And, Byron, I don't want to make you feel self-conscious, but it's great to have you back!" And he threw his arms around the embarrassed Fergie, gave him a hug, and then said, "Father Higgins, lead the way! Men, forward march, on the double!" He turned to the lake, and in a harsh voice he added, "Jarmyn Thanatos, may you rot there forever."

CHAPTER SIXTEEN

"Are you sure you feel all right again, Byron?"

Fergie made a face. "Aw, Prof, that's only the seven hundredth time you've asked me that in the last month. I'm fine!"

It was a warm day in June. School had just ended, and Father Higgins and the professor had taken Fergie, Johnny, and Sarah on a little outing up to Dr. Coote's vacation cottage on Lake Winnepesaukee in New Hampshire. They had been swimming, they had gorged on charcoal-grilled hot dogs and hamburgers and the professor's homemade potato salad, and now they were sitting lazily in lawn chairs, listening to the distant drone of motorboats. The sky was a rich blue, with lots of fluffy white cumulus clouds. The hickory scent of charcoal hung in the warm summer air. From a tall blue-green fir nearby, an enthusiastic mockingbird sang his whole repertoire of bird imitations. It was a perfect afternoon.

"So opposites were the key to Jarmyn Cudbright's magic," Dr. Coote was saying. "He wished to work in secret—and so he had to announce his nefarious doings by the ringing of a bell, real or illusory. He wished to become young—so someone else had to grow old. All opposites, you see."

"Fortunately, Byron liquidated him before he could complete his work," said Professor Childermass.

Dr. Coote nodded. "Opposites again. I should have guessed it would be water. Cudbright believed in astrology, and as he told Nostradamus in his letter, he was an Aries. That is a fire sign. Its opposite, water, would be malevolent toward Cudbright in all aspects."

"No one could have guessed that water would send the old devil to his just reward," said Professor Childermass in a low voice. "It took the poor dying Tommy McCorkle to scratch his warning for us—and even then we didn't understand it and were almost lost. Fortunately, John Michael had a sudden—ahem!—flash of inspiration and saved our bacon. And speaking of loss, has your father adjusted to losing his job at Baxter Motors, Byron?"

Fergie grinned. "I wish I'd been there when he told old man Baxter off. That must have been somethin'! 'I won't work,' Dad said, 'for a liar, a cheat, and a fraud.' An' he walked out, an' some other guys who were fed up with old Baxter clapped their hands! When I heard about it, I felt kinda proud of my old man, y'know? But, yeah, it worked out just fine. Mom an' Dad thought I'd run off because they were fightin' about money, see, an' Dad decided I was worth more to him than the job. I guess it's better for them to think I'd run away than to let 'em know what really happened, so I kinda clammed up about that crazy book and Old Creepy Crawly."

Johnny said, "But Fergie's got more news. His dad has another job already—and a better one."

"Yeah," agreed Fergie. "Turns out that the company Dad traveled for wanted him back. Only not as a salesman. He's gonna be the new district manager. He'll have an office in the First National Bank Building, with a good salary, an' he only has to travel a little now an' then. Mom is lots happier now that he's happy again."

"All's well that ends well," said Father Higgins with a smile. "But it's fortunate for all of us that Jarmyn Thanatos made a crucial mistake. He chose a stubborn, bullheaded, semi-delinquent for his victim instead of some good Catholic boy."

"Hey, no fair," objected Fergie. "Betcha Dixon there could've foxed him just as good as me. Maybe even better, right, John baby?"

"I'd hate to try," said Johnny. "Better you than me, Fergie." He smiled at his friend.

But Sarah was frowning. "I still don't understand how Thanatos kept those mice alive," she said.

Dr. Coote shivered. "Ugh! I hate to think about them.

Well, it's only a guess, but I think that the mice were dead all along. Thanatos preserved their bodies and put a spell on them so they would move and squeak and eat just as if they were alive. But the spell was designed to last for only ten years or so, not eighty. The horrible creature that I had stored away was one of those dead mice. The trouble was that over the years the body had dried out and had become little more than a mouse mummy." He looked pale. "Anyway, I'd rather not talk about it. Mice upset me, and moving, mummified mice upset me even more."

"Well," said Sarah, "*I* was pretty upset that I missed all the excitement. You guys tore off to Maine and left me behind. I don't think that's fair at all."

"We didn't exactly have a lot of time to spare," pointed out the professor. "And you more than did your part when you discovered the tricky magician was heading for Maine. Without you, Fergie would be a gone goose."

"I just hate missing out," complained Sarah.

"You didn't miss anything," Fergie assured her. "I can't remember very much toward the end, except bein' in the dark. But man, was I terrified. He made me read th' whole book, page after page. An' all the time he was complainin' that we had to do it too quick, that I'd only be good for ten or fifteen years, not the sixty or seventy he'd counted on."

"Did you know what he was up to?" asked Sarah.

Fergie hung his head. "Yeah. It was all in the book.

But the more I read, the less I could do about it." He shivered. "How old *was* Thanatos, anyhow?"

Dr. Coote shrugged his thin shoulders. "Who knows? More than three hundred years, at any rate. His motto was *Quis acognoscit mortem, acognoscit artem mortem superantis*. Or, in English, 'He who knows death knows the art of overcoming it.' But you know, I don't believe he had found a true secret of earthly immortality. He renewed himself and was young again time after time, but he lost something of himself each time he did it. Once, say two hundred years ago, he might have been a great and powerful magician, capable of dominating the world. But by the time you met him, he had worn away to little more than an insane desire to prolong his life indefinitely. I think he was quite mad."

"Well, he is now just some rather unsightly sediment at the bottom of a rather polluted pond," retorted Professor Childermass. "And good riddance to him! Attention, all! I have just realized that we still have two perfectly good burgers on the tray next to the grill. Sarah, would you care for one?"

With a smile, she said, "Sorry, Professor. I'd pop if I tried to scarf down one more."

"Fergie? John?"

Johnny shook his head, but with a mischievous grin, Fergie said, "C'mon, Dixon. I dare ya."

"Oh, yeah, Ferguson? Bet I can eat one faster than you can," declared Johnny, returning his grin. "I *double* dare ya!"

Each boy grabbed a burger and began to wolf it

down, drops of mustard and ketchup squirting wildly. The sloppy race wasn't very pretty, but it was funny enough to make Professor Childermass double over with laughter. Sarah made a disgusted face, but she had to laugh too. Everyone joined in, and the joyful sound floated out over the placid mountain lake.

John Bellairs is the critically acclaimed, best-selling author of many Gothic novels, including *The Mummy, the Will, and the Crypt*; *The Lamp from the Warlock's Tomb*; *The Spell of the Sorcerer's Skull*; *The Trolley to Yesterday*; and the novels starring Lewis Barnavelt, Rose Rita Pottinger, and Mrs. Zimmermann. John Bellairs died in 1991.

Brad Strickland wrote *The Bell, the Book, and the Spellbinder* and *The Hand of the Necromancer* and completed several of John Bellairs's novels, including *The Ghost in the Mirror*; *The Vengeance of the Witch-Finder*; *The Doom of the Haunted Opera*; and *The Drum, the Doll, and the Zombie*. He lives in Oakwood, Georgia.